SHELTER ME

A FRAZIER FALLS NOVEL

KELLY COLLINS

BOOK NOOK PRESS

CHAPTER ONE

ELI

I was eager. I was egotistical. I was edgy. Hell, I was Eli Cooper, and that said it all.

"You want a coffee, love?" Alice let the brown-handled pot swing back and forth between her fingers. "You look like you could use a piece of pie too."

From my brother Owen's favorite booth in the corner, I glanced around the diner and could see why he chose it. Nothing happened in Alice's Diner that he wouldn't see.

"Thanks, Alice. I'll take my usual."

"You're a creature of habit." She filled the empty mug.

"And that's a problem?"

"Not for me, but it must get boring for you." She darted off to fetch me a slice of apple pie.

She was right, I was a creature of habit. I loved everything about my simple small-town life in Frazier Falls because it was predictable and perfect, all the way down to Alice's apple pie.

I knew myself, and there were three truths that would never change.

First, I didn't have lofty ambitions. What I wanted was a steady but satisfying job—better if it was stress-free and didn't come with a horrible whip-wielding boss. Setting up Cooper Construction with Owen and pulling in our younger brother Paxton meant we bossed ourselves, or rather Owen bossed us because we allowed it.

Second, I wasn't comfortable with people I didn't know. The best thing about Frazier Falls was I was familiar with everyone.

Third, I could be an asshole. I'd always known this, though most people around me did not. In public, I was perfectly polite and kind to everyone. On my own, or with my brothers, it was another story.

I spent my free time, pretending I knew what everyone was doing, and their reasons for their actions. It was a game Mom and I played to pass the time when I was a child. She called it I Know You. We didn't know anything, but we made up amazing stories about people that entertained us for hours.

The best thing was, nearly fifty percent of the time, I was right, which made it more satisfying. The sly and stupid suggestions about what John Reilly was getting up to behind the doors of his bar, or whether Rachel Wilkes knew how to run a convenience store, or whether Sandra the hairdresser kicked out her no-good husband Paul for drinking or cheating on her, entertained me. With Paul, it was usually one or the other, though my guess was both. I was curious about Lucy and why she was the town gossip, or how Alice managed to stay upbeat despite the work and patience it took to run the diner.

Alice plopped the plate of apple pie in front of me. "I added a scoop of vanilla because you look like you needed it."

Staring at my plate, I wanted to scream, but instead, I looked up and smiled. "Thanks, Alice. You're the best."

When she walked away, I pushed the ice cream to the side

before it could melt into the perfect flaky crust, making it soggy. Damn … even Alice was becoming unpredictable.

With the first bite, I thought about Carla Stevenson. I had to hand it to my brother. He'd found a great woman who happened to come with a nice sibling. The joining of the Stevenson Mill with Cooper Construction was a boon. Liking both the Stevensons was a bonus.

A hand waved in front of my face. "Eli, are you spacing out?" Paxton appeared out of nowhere. "Where did you go?"

I swatted him away as I took another bite before the quickly melting ice cream could touch it.

He slid into the bench across from me and picked up a spoon, taking a big bite of ice cream, which saved me from leaving it on the plate and potentially hurting Alice's feelings.

"I was thinking you should stop flirting with Carla, you moron." No way would I tell him the truth. That I was missing our mother, and the predictability of our lives. Pity parties didn't go over well with the Coopers.

"I don't flirt with her. She belongs to our brother."

I laughed. "You want to tell Carla that marrying Owen will make her his property?" I shook my head. "Make sure you wear a cup when you do. She'll kick your gonads so far up, they'll be stuck in your throat."

"Dude, I'm not telling her anything. Just stop breaking my balls because I like her. She's going to be family."

Paxton had admitted to being half in love with her in high school. He said he wasn't anymore, but I wasn't convinced. There was something about the way he looked after speaking to her that made me think he was either lying to me or lying to himself. Or maybe he was envious of the love our brother had. It was also a possibility that I imagined something that was there for my amusement. No matter what, it got a rise out of my younger brother, which was a perfect distraction for me.

"When are you going to find your own girl?"

"When are you?" he grumbled as he collapsed against the blue pleather seat. "God, I can't believe Carla told you I liked her."

My future sister-in-law, Carla, who everyone called Carl, had impeccable timing. She laughed loudly before she made Pax scoot over. "I think it's cute that you liked me in the first place."

"Stop ganging up on me." Pax's lips stretched into a thin line. "Having one Eli is enough."

Carla sat taller and pressed her palm to her chest. "I've reached Eli levels of mockery? I'm honored."

"You're hilarious," Pax grumbled.

"You realize this was the stuff I was talking about, Pax. You're blushing," I said, causing my brother to roll his eyes and curse under his breath.

Carla looked at me, amused. "I guess we should stop picking on him for now," she looked at Pax and turned back to face me. "Do you have any clue when Owen will get back? He's not picking up his phone."

I glanced at my watch, frowning. My brother was late, but one look out of the window confirmed why. It was snowing hard enough to block the visibility to the stores across the street.

She followed my gaze. "It's really coming down."

"Only in the last couple of minutes. You should head over to Owen's place before the snow keeps you trapped here. Which I wouldn't wish on anyone because the central heating upstairs is down."

"I was thinking you'd turned it off to torture me," Pax complained as he rubbed his hands together. "Or to keep me doing my work instead of falling asleep."

"Did it work?" I asked, raising a curious eyebrow.

"Nah. Now I'm down here getting warm on the outside and freezing my innards by eating your ice cream."

I pushed my plate in his direction. "Eat the rest of it, and then head on home."

"What about you?" Pax asked. "You shouldn't stay either."

I looked at the spreadsheets in front of me. "I'll finish up the finances for the month, and I'll be done."

"But," Pax began, confused, "there are still a few days of January left. Wouldn't it be better to do it all when the month is over?"

I shook my head. "We don't have any projects to work on until February, which you would know if you had read the report I sent you this morning."

My brother let out an exaggerated sigh as he slid his arms into his jacket and nudged Carla out of the booth. "I've got a busy schedule. With winter upon us, the days are shorter, and things are slowing down at work, but picking up in my social circle."

"You mean the *Geriatrics Are Us* fan club?"

"Someday we'll be old too. And I hope there's someone willing to shovel our driveways or mow our lawns."

Carla laughed as she bundled herself into her purple parka. "I'll be leaving too. Do you need a lift, Pax?"

"Nah, I drove here this morning."

She looked at him slack-jawed. "You drove your car? Here? In the snow?"

Pax made a face. "Just because I crashed a few times back in the day doesn't mean I'm an atrocious driver."

"Yes, it does," I interjected. "Carla, please take Paxton home. I don't trust him behind the wheel. He's liable to run over the very people he helps."

Pax swore at me but accepted the order. When it came down to it, he knew as well as I did, he'd barely made it to the office alive this morning. He had failed to change the tires on his car for the snow this year. He was convinced it would clear up in a day or two like it always did.

However, this winter had arrived with a vengeance and brought the heaviest snowfall Frazier Falls had seen in thirty years. Blankets of the white stuff kept the masses inside.

I smiled to myself as Pax and Carla left Alice's Diner, leaving me in blessed silence. It only took fifteen minutes to finish up the report I'd been working on, but something was keeping me from heading home. I didn't know what. Maybe it was because my house was empty.

There was something satisfying about working in the peace and quiet of an empty office or the corner of the diner, but going home to an unoccupied house was another feeling entirely.

I wasn't lonely. I wasn't. Getting the fire going in my living room, cooking dinner, and sitting down with a beer to watch a movie while the snow continued to fall sounded great, but in order to do that, I had to first set foot inside a cold, empty house, and then wait for it to become welcoming.

Shit ... maybe I *was* lonely. The idea of someone at home waiting for me sounded wonderful.

The reality was, even if I were to find a girlfriend, asking her to get a fire going for my return was ludicrous—and old-fashioned. It was right up there with telling a woman she was a man's property.

The way things worked between my mother and father was different from how couples behaved these days. The Cooper household had been warm and welcoming because of Mom. I relished the memories of my childhood in winter. A blazing fire. Hot cocoa. Cookies straight from the oven. My mother's smile. That was the best. The thing I missed the most.

I shook my head; I wasn't twelve anymore. I was thirty-four and quickly approaching thirty-five. Hell, I was certain I was more of an adult than Owen was half the time. He still kept secrets like his propensity for panic attacks. Only a few months ago, he had a complete meltdown in public at his architecture conference. Sometimes I felt like the older brother. Though I took comfort in knowing he was doing much better now, I couldn't stop worrying, regardless.

"Hey, where is everyone?" Owen called out. I looked up to see him entering the diner. He was covered in snow. His boots were packed with the stuff, insulating the sound of his footsteps when he walked inside. The cold wind breezed past the open door, bringing with it a flurry of snowflakes.

"Close the door," Alice called from the counter. "Were you born in a barn?"

He grinned and shut it, though it barely made a sound through all the snow gathered around the frame.

"It's getting bad out there."

"That's why everyone went home," I said. "Pax came in late because of it."

"He was up at the mill this morning," Owen moved toward the booth. "Then he went into town to help out Lucy Rogers and John Reilly."

"Why did John need help?"

"You honestly think he could unload all the stock in this weather? The kegs would be half-frozen. Pax, not wanting to go to Huck's if John had to close the bar, helped him out."

"How selfless of him," I said with a measure of sarcasm. "By the way, Carla came by earlier."

His eyes lit up. "When did she leave?"

"About ten minutes ago. I told her to go straight to your place."

"Thanks, Eli. Do you need help with anything?" I could tell he was hoping the answer would be a resounding no.

I shook my head, smiling. "I'm about to head out myself. Did you take the truck?"

"I did. Do you want a lift home? I don't think your car will cut it in this weather."

"I could take the company truck."

"Don't be silly. Grab your jacket, and we'll swing by Wilkes' convenience store for beer."

"I'm not going to your place to drink."

He looked at me. "Doesn't mean you won't want some for yourself."

"Very true. But nah, take me straight home if that's okay."

I paid the bill and shrugged on my jacket. We dashed through the falling snow in a hurry to get to my house so Owen could get home to Carla.

I reasoned that I didn't have space in my life for a girlfriend, even if I had wanted one. The business and my brothers were enough to handle. And yet, when I set foot in my cold, empty house, I felt hollow.

CHAPTER TWO

EMILY

"Ma, if I've said it once I've said it a thousand times, of all the places in the world to move to, why did you move here?"

"Because the air is clean, the people are nice, and it's quiet."

"What you did was choose someplace like Ireland in a different country."

"Not really, the accent's all wrong. But you know … that sounds tempting—"

"No," I interrupted, suppressing a shudder, "don't even joke about going back. You hated small-town life, and yet, came to Frazier Falls like you were a moth, and the town was a flame."

"Emily, you adored Ireland until we moved to California."

"Exactly—until—but I'd never go back now that I know there's something else out there. This place isn't much better than Ardmore."

"Oh, come now, sweetheart, the snow is beautiful. And if you would only visit in the summer, you'd see it's lovelier here than California."

I cringed at the thought. When Mom and I had moved to the United States, I'd waved my miserable existence in Ardmore, Ireland, goodbye. The village I'd lived in had barely over three hundred people—three hundred people that never stopped talking about my father's philandering. Even though Frazier Falls had closer to five thousand, somehow, the place felt exactly the same. Small. Cramped. Full of busybodies. There was nothing to do for anyone over the age of five or under seventy.

It was fine for Mom. She had turned seventy last year but had moved to Frazier Falls fifteen years prior when I'd started my freshman year at Berkeley. She loved it as much as I loathed it.

I should have been in California, getting past the post-New Year work slump and preparing for a busy February, but Mom was sick. Her health had been iffy for a few years, and now it was getting worse. I'd taken time off from work since the New Year. My plan was to get her to move to California, so she'd be close, and I could take care of her.

"You know, Emily," Mom continued as if I wasn't in a terrible mood already. "If you tried to make a couple of friends here, you wouldn't be as lonely when you visited."

"I'm not in high school, Ma. I'm thirty-three."

"Yes, and friendless."

"I have lots of friends back in Los Angeles, which is where I'll be next week. There's really no point making an effort."

A flash of sadness crossed her eyes, and I immediately felt awful. Mom was digging in her heels. We were both jockeying for the same outcome. She wanted me to stay, and I wanted her to go.

"I love being with you, but you know I have to go back. My life is there. I'm a city girl. Besides, it pays the bills." I raised a brow, hoping she wouldn't make me point out that my income helped her too. It paid the medical bills her insurance didn't cover and put a new roof over her head when the old one leaked.

My mom laughed. "If the weather keeps up like this, you won't be going anywhere until spring, Miss Flanagan."

There were some things that would make the list of my worst nightmares. Walking into a room full of spiders was one. Having to eat lentils for the rest of my life would be another. Getting snowed in was the worst. Talking about it almost made it possible, so I shifted the conversation.

The lights flickered but stayed on. "I'm worried the power is going to cut out at any moment. I don't want that happening when I leave next week. Is there anyone you can get to come over and make sure the backup generator is running when I'm gone?"

"Sweetheart"—the oxygen tank whirred and hissed with each breath—"there's no backup generator. If the power goes out, I'll have to rely on candles and firewood until it comes back on."

"Ma." This information didn't ease my worry. Candles and firewood would never cut it. I needed to add a backup generator to my list of things to buy.

"What?"

"This is why you're not recovering. If you have no backup generator then—"

My mom raised her hands in the air. "Although this may be the worst winter to hit Colorado in 30 years, I have never been without power from a snowstorm for longer than an hour."Global warming, my arse."

"You say that like global warming is a conspiracy instead of an actual thing."

"God. You and your geography."

"Well, it is what I studied for years."

"I thought you were a city planner or something."

"Which is a pretty standard geography career."

She frowned. "I thought geography was about rocks?"

"That's geology. Geography covers more than capital cities and global warming."

Mom waved a hand. "As long as you like it."

When I was growing up, I dreamed of being a ballerina. Turned out, I lacked rhythm, and I liked Jaffa cakes too much. I had aspirations of being a meteorologist for a while, but that didn't pan out either. City planning paid the bills and bought me great shoes. "I like it."

Mom sighed. "I wish you had kept on trying to become a weather girl—"

"A meteorologist—"

"Your red hair would look pretty on camera, Emily."

"Sure, that's the only reason I wanted to do it. To look pretty on camera."

"Being on the telly could be a perk. I'm sure you'd have found a boyfriend much faster if you—"

I held up my hand. "Don't start."

"I never meet any of your boyfriends anymore. Do you ever plan to settle down?"

"It's not my number one priority."

"But you're thirty-three."

I arched my right brow. "And?"

"I don't get it. With your beautiful hair, and your lovely accent —you know they all go mad for an Irish accent over here—I don't understand why a man hasn't tried to marry you."

"Who's saying a man hasn't?"

Mom immediately perked up. "Who?"

"Remember Kyle?"

"I do. What ever happened there? All you said was you'd outgrown him, but you never mentioned a proposal."

"It was five years ago, and when I got the job in Los Angeles. Kyle and I were living in that apartment near Berkeley. He gave me an ultimatum. I had to choose between him or the job." She saw the wistful look of a woman who wanted grandchildren. "You can put away that look of hope and stop generating a guest list in your head."

She tutted as if my being single was a true tragedy, and a more pressing matter than her ailing health.

"Sometimes, I blame myself, sweetheart. If your da—"

"Da left when I was twelve, and it wasn't your fault. Leave it alone."

"He left because I wouldn't go with him."

"He left because he was a philanderer and was on the kill list of most men and women in Ardmore. You knew if you had gone with him, it would have been more of the same." She growled. "Men and their ultimatums. Da backed you into a corner, and you made the right choice. I'll never allow a man to influence my choices."

I knew I'd come across as short-tempered, but I was fed up with her thinking that if the son of a bitch she'd called her husband had only stuck around, then I'd be well-rounded.

The last thing I'd needed in my life was a womanizing drunk sticking around during my teen years. Ma moving the two of us to the United States was the best decision she'd ever made. Although, it would have been nice to see him once more, to prove that we didn't need a man in our life to make it perfect. I was grateful he'd left us, and grateful we'd left the small-town. I now lived in the land of opportunity, and I was taking the proverbial bull by the horns—or at least trying to.

The living room filled with silence for a few moments. Both of us obviously reflecting on the people from our past.

"I wish Mary was here," I finally said.

"You and me both, sweetheart."

Mary had been my mother's best friend. She'd moved to California five years before my mom had moved us. She'd been half the reason we left Ireland. The two of them were thick as thieves and lived three glorious years in Northern California before seeking out a quieter life in Frazier Falls.

"I'd always thought she'd outlive me," Mom said with a sad voice. She stared out the window at the snow, which was barely visible behind the condensation-clouded glass. "I mean, I smoked twenty a day. She never touched a cigarette. I put down a pint a night. She never drank. Mary was the pinnacle of health."

"Healthy people have heart attacks too."

"But it … it isn't fair. Sometimes, I wish I'd hurry up and—"

My heart sank into the pit of my stomach. "Don't. Don't even think of finishing that sentence."

"Look at me, Emily," she said bleakly, gesturing toward the oxygen tank by the side of the sofa. A bad case of pneumonia had sucked the energy from her lungs. When we thought she'd kicked the virus, it came back with a vengeance.

The cold weather didn't help any. It scratched and clawed inside of her, making breathing difficult. She could barely leave the house with the weather this bad.

"Ma, just do what you're supposed to, and you'll be fine. Hell, you're Irish, and stubborn, which means you'll outlive all of us." God, I hoped so.

I wandered into the kitchen and checked the fridge and pantry. We were running low on supplies. I'd been appalled upon arriving to discover she'd been eating mostly ready-made meals and canned food. The memory burned me up inside.

I'd stocked the kitchen with everything I could think of in order to cook her three solid meals a day, which to my relief, had improved her health.

Worry filled me. If my cooking was helping her get better, then that meant when I left, she'd get worse. My stomach churned at the thought.

Colorado's weather was too extreme for her. She needed mild, comfortable, and safe. She needed a clean house and good food and engaging company. She needed to get back to California.

"Ma, I'm going to have to go to that convenience store."

"In this weather? Emily, it's awful outside."

"Unless you want to eat dry cereal for dinner, then you'll have to let me go."

The oxygen tank hissed and moaned with each labored breath. "I don't suppose we could have some wine?"

I shook my head. "Not when you're on the tank and meds. If the weather lets up, and your breathing improves, we can talk about it."

"Remember when we enjoyed a few drinks in the pubs when we went back to visit your grandparents? You were eighteen then."

"Oh, God, that was crazy, drinking with Grandad," I giggled. "He pickled himself on a daily basis."

"Drank like a fish, my da."

And there was that sad look on Mom's face again—the same expression she wore when talking about Mary. Her best friend was gone, her parents were gone, and her friends back in Ardmore were all beginning to succumb to disease and old age.

Mom was lonely. Truly lonely. My tongue felt too thick to form words, but I pasted on a smile, and forced a few out. "I won't be long if I can help it. Love you."

"You too, sweetheart."

Even after wrapping up in two sweaters, my mother's massive down jacket, a scarf, and thick gloves, the wind and snow were bitterly cold. It bit and pinched at my face as I pulled the material up higher and ran for the car.

By the time I closed the door and started the engine, my teeth were chattering.

"This place is horrible," I muttered as I struggled out of my gloves to turn on the heater, sighing in relief when a wave of warm air washed over my exposed skin.

I wasn't going to give up trying to persuade Mom to move back to California. It was better for both of us. As I inched toward the tiny market, my worry and irritation grew exponentially. How was I supposed to live a thousand miles away and keep an eye on my mom?

By the time I walked into Wilkes Corner Store, I was like a shaken pop can ready to explode.

CHAPTER THREE

ELI

The wind and snow roared past my window, and I was out of milk.

In truth, I was out of everything.

I had two choices, stay home and starve, or bundle up and brave the storm.

Going outside was the last thing I wanted to do, given the fact that I had only recently gotten back home. I made the decision easier, by upping the temperature on the heating so my house would be a hell of a lot warmer when I returned.

With little sunlight to power the solar panels, I had to use energy from the grid. While this was offset by the fact that the grid paid me for the energy my solar panels added to it during the summer, it still irritated me. I liked being self-supporting. It was one of the beautiful things about the Green House Project, though I wouldn't admit that to Owen.

This winter was cold—so cold that I had used far more energy than I would have otherwise liked. And yet, I wasn't an idiot.

There was no way I would risk starting a fire and leave it to get hot while I went to buy food.

"I must be insane," I murmured as I steeled myself to leave my house. Owen had driven me home, which meant I had to walk. Luckily, Wilkes Corner Store was a couple of minutes from my front door.

It took me closer to ten minutes to trudge through the storm, cursing the wind every time it buffeted me back. When I walked inside, I was more than surprised to find Pax behind the counter.

"What the hell are you doing here? I thought Carla took you home." I spluttered when I entered the warmth of the building.

"You think Rachel could keep the place open in this weather? I had Carla drop me by her house, and I grabbed the keys and Rachel's SUV."

He looked at me pointedly. Rachel Wilkes was nearing seventy. She'd be at home instead of struggling to get to and from work.

I brushed the snow from my jacket. The flakes floated around me like a mini indoor storm.

"She needs to get regular staff in here."

"I think she will. This winter has shaken her up. The poor thing nearly fell on the ice yesterday."

"That's not good. Where was the ice? I thought the roads had been salted?"

"In front of her house. I salted it for her this morning, but it'll be frozen over again by now."

"You're right. Please tell me you're going to get yourself home soon. It's rotten outside."

He looked at the store's clock. "I'm closing at six. You're lucky you came by when you did. I wanted to stay open for those that planned poorly." He gave me a knowing look.

"Yes, I definitely consider having to go through this storm on foot to buy food, so I don't starve, lucky."

Though Pax was usually pretty quiet around people, he was fairly outspoken with his family. As outspoken as Pax could be, which wasn't saying much.

I left my brother to walk up and down the aisles to find everything I needed along with anything else that struck me as a good idea to pick up in case Wilkes' stayed closed for a few days. I grabbed canned tomatoes and other vegetables. Ultra-heat-treated, long shelf-life milk. Chocolate. Beer. It was about the time my shopping cart became full of more food and drink than I could carry back that I distinctly regretted not taking Owen up on his offer to stop when I'd been in his truck.

"You're such an idiot," I grumbled as I walked past an unfamiliar woman investigating the small selection of fresh fruit and vegetables.

"Excuse me?" She narrowed her eyes.

"Oh, I apologize." I tried to keep my tone indifferent. "I was talking to myself."

"Do that often?" she asked before returning her gaze to a pair of sad-looking potatoes. "What's with this damn place? No fruits or vegetables. People talk to themselves. The weather is the worst."

"I'd like to point out that you're doing exactly the same thing." Going by the woman's Irish accent, I could only assume she was in some way related to old Judy Flanagan.

"Excuse me?"

"You say that a lot."

"And you seem to enjoy interrupting my thoughts."

"Only pointing out the facts." I reached over her and grabbed the last onion, tossing it into my basket and moving forward.

"I was going to take that," she called after me.

"Now it's gone." I was too tired to engage in a prickly conversation with a woman I didn't know, especially given the walk through a freezing storm I'd have to face to get home.

"I hate small towns."

She tossed her red hair over her shoulder; melted snowflakes flew out to hit me like tiny stinging bees.

"What's your problem, Miss ...?"

"None of your business."

"Have it your way. If you need potatoes, there should be some in the back. Might even be an onion or two. Ask Pax at the front counter. He's covering for the owner. If you're extra nice, he might bring you over a sack."

Her eyes blinked in bewilderment. "Nice? Why are you being nice after being so rude?"

"Because I wasn't being rude," I said as I walked toward the frozen section. "Just putting my nose where it doesn't belong. It's a small-town problem. Have a lovely day." I said with a tone that could only be considered unfriendly.

"That was—"

"Yes, that was rude," I interrupted, glancing over my shoulder to see her looking at me. Her jaw clenched so tight I swear I heard a molar crack.

Ten minutes later, I'd paid for my groceries and stood talking to Pax in sheer procrastination. I absolutely didn't want to go outside. Even when the woman from the fresh produce aisle came over to pay for her food, I didn't budge. When she fired me several withering looks that could have cooked me alive, I remained fixed in my position.

However, when she struggled at the door, I heard my mom's voice telling me to be a gentleman. I grabbed my bags and said goodbye to Pax, then pushed open the door. She startled at my presence and juggled her shopping bags successfully. My chivalry earned me another glare.

"You're welcome," I parroted in a terrible impersonation of her accent.

She twisted around, no doubt intending to fire off a response, but in doing so, she slipped on the icy parking lot and lost her balance.

Without thinking, I dropped my bags and rushed over, catching her before her head would have hit the concrete.

Through clouds of frosted breath, and in the artificial glow of the streetlights, I saw the color of her eyes, and I was momentarily stunned into silence.

They were the most beautiful shade of green I'd ever seen—the exact color of the Frazier Firs the town was named after.

"Let me go." She twisted out of my hold and scrambled to her feet.

I could hardly believe my ears. "I just saved you at the expense of my own groceries, and all you can say is 'let me go'?"

"You're the reason I fell in the first place."

I let out a growl. "If somebody had minded their manners and thanked me for opening the door—"

"I never asked you to."

"Fine. You know what? I'm done trying to be nice." I took a shot in the dark. "I hope you don't treat your mother this way."

She looked as if she were about to fling another insult at me, but she paled. "What do you know about my ma?"

My assumption was correct. She was, indeed, Judy Flanagan's daughter. While she had gotten her mother's red hair, she missed out on her pleasant demeanor. "Only that Judy is a wonderful woman. Lord give her strength being stuck in a house with you all winter."

"You're a dick."

"No, I'm Eli Cooper."

Muttering a complaint to myself, I turned my back on her as I peered through the snow to locate my groceries. Several cans had rolled out, but most of my shopping had stayed within the confines of the bags, which were now topped with snow. Another thing I could add to the growing list of shitty things that had happened to me in the past hour.

"I don't," the woman called out to me over the roar of the wind.

I picked up my bags and whipped around to look at her. "You don't what?"

"Talk to my ma like that. Clearly you know her. How—how has she been the past few months?"

I shook my head in disbelief. "Seems like something her daughter should know."

She stomped on her foot, but the packed snow ate up the sounds of her effort. "Why are you judging me?"

"I call it how I see it." I tossed a runaway can back into my bag and readjusted the weight in my arms.

Her brows lowered and knitted together. "You small-town folk are all alike. You only see what you want to see. Next thing I know, there will be all kinds of rumors about Judy's rotten daughter."

"You're something, aren't you? You ask me not to judge you, and yet you pass judgment on me and everyone else who lives here."

With her eyebrows knitted together, she shook her head. "Forget it. Forget I asked you anything."

I considered what to say next. This was a no-win situation. "Tell you what," I began, "I'll let you know if you tell me your name."

She crossed her arms. "Seriously? You're going to bribe a girl in a snowstorm. I know she's sick, but I don't know if she's being completely honest with me?"

"You're not a girl. You're a grown woman who should know the state of her mother's health already." I tugged my collar higher up my neck. "I only wanted to know your name, but I could visit and ask your mom instead."

"Ugh, bloody busybody," she grumbled. "For your information, I ask her all the time about her health, and she tells me she's fine."

The word bloody sounded exquisite in her accent, which seemed to have grown more pronounced the more worked up she'd gotten.

"You want to know about your mom? I'll need a name."

She let out a resigned breath. "Emily."

"Emily?"

"My name. It's Emily. Now, how has she been?"

"Not great," I admitted. "We had a hot summer, which quickly turned into a harsh winter. We hardly got any fall at all. We don't see her in Reilly's anymore."

"We?"

"Me and my brothers. We used to drive her home if she'd had one too many."

Emily looked uncomfortably at the ground. "Thank you."

"What was that?" I leaned in, feigning temporary deafness as I held a cupped hand up to my near-frozen ear.

"Thank you," she burst out. "God, you're impossible."

"I've been told." I pulled the bags to my chest, hoping they'd insulate me from the cold. "You get home safely."

She rolled her eyes, then returned to her car without another word.

"Didn't even offer to drive me home." I held the bags tightly and trudged slowly back.

When I arrived, I all but fell through my front door. The central heating, a miracle of modern ingenuity, warmed my frozen skin as I shed layers of clothing and put away my purchases. I didn't have the energy to cook after my ordeal, so I made do with a microwave pizza and a bottle of beer.

I flopped on my sofa and flicked through the channels until I came across a show with an Irish actress who reminded me of the red-haired vixen from the market.

"Emily Flanagan," I murmured.

It was time to learn everything I could about the newest, meanest girl in town.

CHAPTER FOUR

EMILY

The sound of my cell phone buzzing was a welcome relief in the silence of Mom's living room. She was asleep, and I was using the central heating instead of the fireplace for warmth. I told myself it was because it seemed ridiculous to build a fire when I could have a warm house at the click of a button, but in reality, it was because I had never been able to start a lasting fire in my life.

I loved the crackling, sparking noise like the bonfires they used to build on Guy Fawkes Night back in Ardmore. My mom used to joke that it was silly for the village to celebrate a British tradition, but there was something inherently satisfying about the whole affair. As my grandfather used to point out, there was nothing wrong with celebrating everything.

It didn't matter that I was Irish and not English. A giant bonfire burning away, sending plumes of smoke fifteen feet into the clear and frosty night sky was mesmerizing. There were other memories associated with it—toffee apples, plastic cups of soup, fireworks, and running around with the six other children in the village. It had been magical.

Now, as an adult who knew better, the memory was spoiled by how cold I got by standing around waiting for the fireworks, or how often the whole festival was canceled because it rained, which happened a lot. In reality, there were only one or two good bonfire nights that I had witnessed in my life, but they'd left a lasting memory.

They still stuck with me, grinding away at my consciousness until all I wanted to see in the living room fireplace was an inferno, and so I gave it a try.

Fifteen minutes later, I was covered in soot, with a sorry excuse for a flame struggling amidst the kindling and firewood.

"What was it Grandad told me?" I murmured. "Don't suffocate it? What does that even mean?"

I strategically placed twists of paper here and there to attract the flame. It was still cold. Something I'd never associated with a fiery lick of heat before. No doubt, it needed time to build up. Patience was a virtue I'd always struggled to master.

Thoughts of my mother, and how happy she would be when she woke to see a roaring fire, filled my head. I grinned merely thinking about it. It was a simple thing, but she was too sick to get on her knees and start one up herself. With her compromised lungs, the smoke would be a killer.

Twenty minutes later, the fire seemed to be doing much better. It was finally getting warm. Reasonably convinced that it would do its own thing now, I settled into the corner of the sofa with a blanket and my cell phone, content to torture myself with the social media updates of my friends all happily living their lives in Los Angeles. I nearly dropped the damn thing when it buzzed in my hand.

My best friend, Sadie, was calling.

"God, am I glad you rang," I immediately blurted out. "I'm

going absolutely batshit crazy over here in the backwoods of the bloody beyond. It's—"

"Woah, slow down there, Irish," Sadie joked. "Your accent is showing, and I can barely understand a word you're saying."

I took a deep breath, let my heart slow down, then spoke with a far more painstakingly crafted, neutral voice. "Sorry. You know how it is when I only have my mom for company."

"Not made any friends there?"

"I hope you're joking."

"Not found anyone down at the local bar to hang with? Canoodle with?"

"There is no canoodling happening here. The thought makes me cringe. Even if there was someone to meet—which there isn't—it would be impossible because the weather is horrific."

"Like planes are canceled horrific?"

"Yep," I nodded my head in misery, "At least for now. I'm hoping it clears up by next week so I can get back to work. I'm out of vacation time, and I can't see the boss man giving me extra comp time." It was hard to believe I'd spent the month of January in Frazier Falls. "I've been gone too long by about thirty days."

"Aw, Flanagan, it can't be that bad."

"You say that, but you have no idea how awful people can be. You're so lucky you've always lived in a city where people stay to themselves and mind their business and manners."

"Sounds like you had an encounter."

"Hardly." I jumped in fright when the fire let out a loud pop. It was merely a log splitting in two, but scary, regardless. Once the sparks settled, the flames continued to happily dance away.

"Tell me who has you burning inside?"

"Burning implies a level of passion for a person worth heating up over, which he isn't."

"Okay, now I'm curious," Sadie said. "Who is he?"

That's what she wanted to know. "He was arrogant as hell and went on to tell me I was the one being awful. In the end, he told me my ma deserved better than me."

She laughed. "Sounds like you've met your match. How old is he? Is he hot?"

"Don't you care how torturous it is for me to be here?"

"Yes, but this is the closest thing to gossip you've had to tell me since you left. You've gotta spill. It's your responsibility as my best friend to entertain me."

I checked the time on my mother's ancient grandfather clock, which had survived the trip from Ireland to become the only possession she had left from her old life.

"Shouldn't you be working? It's barely four."

"Yes, but I'm bored. You know we can't do anything until you come back and get our project plans approved. At this rate, that will be February. Give me something to talk about until then."

I laughed quietly. "Fine. You win. The guy couldn't have been much older than me. And he was hot as hell, which makes him more annoying."

Sadie let out an ooh of interest. "Ooh, what did he look like? Give me details."

"Legit tall, dark, and handsome. Blue eyes, I think."

"You think?"

"I was trying not to be obvious when I checked him out in the store, given that we were arguing. It was dark in the parking lot when we had our next encounter, so I'm not sure."

"What happened in the parking lot?"

I growled. "I slipped on the ice and fell. He caught me."

"Emily, that's not arrogant. He was being chivalrous, and that's a rarity these days. You need to jump on this guy pronto. It's not like you're going to be around long enough for an actual relationship, so who gives a crap if he's slightly unpleasant? In this case, hot trumps everything."

"All you want are the dirty details."

"Absolutely! At a minimum, you need to get me a photo of him."

"Sorry, no can do. I'm hoping I'll somehow never see him again, though it seems like his brother works in the only convenience store in town, so knowing my luck, we'll run into each other again."

"He has a brother? Is he hot, too? He might be nicer … you never know."

"You're awful. But yeah, he was pretty damn good-looking too."

"God, it's not fair. Clearly, all the handsome guys have left Los Angeles and moved to Frazier Falls."

"Hardly," I laughed. "Most of the male population here are in diapers, both young and old. I did get his name, though."

"Which is?"

I paused for a moment to remember. "Eli. Eli Cooper."

"Give me two seconds."

"For what?"

My phone buzzed a few seconds later. Sadie had sent me a photo—of Eli.

"Did you social media stalk him?"

"It's one of my many superpowers. That's him, right?"

I didn't want to say yes, but it was him—every tall, dark, and brooding bit of him. "Yep," I said reluctantly. "That's him."

"Oh my God, he's gorgeous. Seriously, get yourself on his profile now. And who is—Christ almighty,—he has two brothers, and they're all stupidly hot. That's so unfair." There was a moment of silence followed by an ear-piercing squeal. "And a soon-to-be brother-in-law, too. Who's also handsome. That means one of them is getting married. Not Eli, though, so I guess you're in luck."

"Stop planning my life. You're being creepy."

"And you're being impossible."

"Like you said, I'll be leaving soon. Who cares how many brothers this guy has, or who's getting married?"

"You should, so you can get in there for some fun before you fly back. God knows you need it."

"Like I said, if luck is on my side, I'll never see this Eli guy or his brothers again. I'm here for my ma. Speaking of …" I paused when I heard the sound of footsteps in the hallway. "It sounds like she's up. I better go. Thanks for calling and giving me a few moments of normalcy."

"Any time. I mean it. Call me any time. Preferably during work, because I need the distraction."

"I don't know how you keep your job."

"Me either," Sadie laughed. "You love me, and you know it, Flanagan."

"As much as I hate to admit it, I do. Go back to work."

"Overrated." She sighed. "Go find that guy and do the same."

"Sadie—"

But the call ended with a click, leaving my protest unfinished as my mom wheeled her oxygen tank to the living room. The flickering fire lit up her eyes.

"Emily, sweetheart, you have no idea how lovely it is to see a fire."

I stood up and led her to the corner of the sofa, arranging her oxygen tank down by her feet as I put a blanket over her lap. "Do you want some tea, Ma?"

"Yes, please. A glass of wine sounds better, but I'll settle for tea"

"If you can't have alcohol, the least I can do is make you something full of caffeine."

Mom chuckled, but it came out more like a cough.

"Is Earl Grey okay?" I asked from the kitchen. "That convenience store was out of normal tea bags yesterday."

"That works. Milk and—"

"Two sugars," I finished for her. "I know."

I found a chocolate bar in the cupboard to go along with the tea. It wasn't a perfect pairing, but it would do. Oh, to have a packet of good, old-fashioned digestive biscuits would have been perfect. Sometimes, I could admit that there were things about Ireland that I missed in America. Proper biscuits were one of them.

When I returned to the living room with tea, my mother sighed in appreciation as she took the cup from my hand. She inhaled the steam with a smile on her face.

"Nothing like a good cup of tea."

"I can't attest to it being any good, but it's still tea."

There was silence for a minute or two as we ate and drank, then I located the television remote and found her favorite channel.

"Who was that on the phone?" she asked.

"It was Sadie. She was checking in to see how things were going."

"I take it you told her things were terrible?"

"Hmm ... maybe."

"You know, one day, you might rediscover those small-town roots of yours and realize you love this place."

I made a face. "It's not likely. Frazier Falls doesn't have much to offer me." What I wanted to say was Frazier Falls wouldn't pay for the utilities or put food on the table. I did that by working in Los Angeles.

"Hard to believe you made do with three hundred folks once upon a time."

"Yep, seems unthinkable now." After another moment of silence, I turned to face her. "Do you miss it? Ardmore, I mean?"

"Oh, no. Not at all," mom laughed. "The weather was awful, and the MacLellans' were the worst gossipers in town. Your da wasn't always a good guy, but the stories they told about him grew taller each time. I'm glad we moved. Frazier Falls seems like the happy medium between a tiny village like ours and a big city. I'm happy here."

"What can I do to persuade you to move back to Los Angeles?"

Mom frowned. "Emily, please stop trying to get me to move closer to you. I want to enjoy what I have left of my life. I can't do that in California. It's too crowded. Too much everything."

"I know." She was right. It was all those things, but it was home.

I let out a sigh of resignation. I'd always known I got my stubbornness from my mother, but now it was coming back to bite me. If I couldn't convince her to come back with me, then that meant …

No. Don't even think about it. You can't move here. No job. No hope. No life.

The thought was enough to send shivers down my spine.

I would never, even if my life depended on it, move to Frazier Falls. But what if Ma's life depended on it?

CHAPTER FIVE

ELI

The snow had finally let up enough that my brothers and I could head out for our usual Friday drinks at Reilly's. It couldn't have come at a better time. I was certain Pax was on his way to suffering from full-on cabin fever because he'd said at least a hundred words in the last ten minutes.

"And then John Reilly had the gall to say I'd been flirting with his wife. I didn't even talk to her—I smiled, and somehow I was flirting."

"Pax," Owen muttered. "Shut. Up."

I glanced at him, surprised. He shrugged his shoulders. "He's been staying with me all week, and he's driving me crazy."

"I was trying to bond," Paxton complained. "I thought being snowed in together would do the trick, but now I'm tired of the snow and Owen."

"Stop whining," I said.

Pax glowered at me. "It's never been this bad. At least not since I could remember, which means I was really young during the last massive snowstorm. This is the worst winter I've had to survive in my entire life."

"It's not like Eli and I remember that much, either," Owen chimed in. "I was six. All I remember is staying inside a lot. School was canceled." He pumped his fist in the air. "That was a bonus."

"And yet, we keep our office open even though we have no orders. What's up with that?" Pax complained.

"If it makes you feel better,"—I got up to buy another round —"we've got all of next week off. No need to go in until the second week of February."

"Except for me and Rich," Owen added. "We're visiting a prospective site for the Green House apartments on Tuesday, weather permitting."

"You should take Carla, or she'll get jealous," Pax said. "She could start thinking you like Rich more than her. You spend more time with him, after all."

We all laughed, but Owen waved a hand dismissively.

"I'm not sleeping with Rich. Besides, Carla doesn't like flying when the weather's bad."

"How far is the site? Can you drive?"

"I don't know, Pax—can I drive to Germany?"

"Germany?" Pax sputtered. "Wow, you're getting your name out there."

"Our name," he said.

"That's enough reason for another round." I looked from brother to brother. "Same?"

Owen shook his head. "Swap me over to vodka and cranberry juice. Can't be drinking beer all night."

"That's called getting old," I remarked.

"Eli, you're only two years younger than me."

"Yep, and that means I have two more years of drinking beer." I lifted my near-empty mug. "Cheers."

Leaving my brothers to head to the bar, I signaled Ruthie, the barmaid, that I was ready to order. She put down her phone and smiled.

"What will it be, Eli?"

I laid a twenty on the table. "That was quite the smile. What were you looking at on your phone?"

She blushed. It was adorable against her strawberry-blond hair and the spray of freckles across her nose.

"I may have a date with a guy from the next town over." She looked out the window. "If this snow ever lets up."

"Lord knows you need to get away from the men in Frazier Falls," I half-joked.

She made a face. "I can't possibly do much worse than your brother."

Before Owen had gotten serious with Carla, he'd taken Ruthie on a disastrous first date. Their only date. While the two of them weren't what you'd call friends, Ruthie was pleasant to all of us again.

She nodded to the group. "What are you guys drinking? John told me your drinks are on the house tonight because Pax helped him out with the deliveries yesterday."

"My brother is a saint." I had to hand it to Paxton, his willingness to help everyone sure paid off for all of us. "Make it two beers and a vodka cranberry easy on the vodka."

"Is that for Owen?"

I glanced at her, surprised. "How'd you know?"

"He usually changes after a few beers," she replied as she rummaged around behind the bar to make our drinks. "Maybe Carla can convince him that beer before liquor will make him sicker."

"That almost sounds like you care, Ruthie."

"Almost." She trayed the drinks and slid them forward. "Take these to your table, and let me go back to texting this guy in peace."

"Say no more." I dropped the twenty into her tip jar. If we weren't paying for drinks all night, then it was the least I could do. She saw the Jackson sticking out of the jar and smiled.

"Everyone says Owen's the gentleman, but I'd say it's you."

"It's all a front. I'm a complete fraud."

"I can believe that."

I laughed the comment off as I took the drinks back to my brothers, who were looking behind me with curious glances.

"What's wrong?" I sat down and looked in the direction of their stares. Emily Flanagan had entered Reilly's with an unsure look on her face.

"Who's that?" Owen asked.

"I think she's Judy Flanagan's niece or daughter or something," Paxton said.

"Daughter," I blurted. "Her name's Emily."

Owen stared at me. "How could you possibly know that? Have you met her?"

Pax handed out the drinks. "At the grocery store. They were having a cat-fight in Wilkes' yesterday."

I looked at him with annoyance. "We were not. She's a typical spoiled city girl."

"Her mom's nice," Pax broke in.

"Judy's kindness didn't rub off on her daughter." I grabbed my beer and took a long drink and took another look. She might not have been nice, but she sure was pretty.

"I didn't hear you get her name in the store," Pax said. "She wouldn't even look at you." He shook his head.

"That's not true; she shot daggers my way."

Owen laughed. "She hated you before she gave you her name? Aw, Eli, she hurt your feelings? No wonder you don't like her."

"It wasn't like that, and you know it." I chanced another look at her. I didn't know why, but I was pulled in her direction. Something about her drew me in. Could it be because she had acted like I didn't exist?

"So how did you get her name? You stalk her? Go ask her mom?"

"Shut the hell up, Pax."

"See?" Owen pointed to Pax. "Imagine that annoying voice all week." He sipped his drink and turned my way. "You still haven't said how you got her to tell you her name."

"She nearly fell in the parking lot," I explained. "I caught her going down. To be honest, it was my fault because I startled her, but I can't say she didn't deserve it. She told me her name after that."

"Your epic love story has finally begun," Owen joked.

"No way. She and I are like dogs and cats. Her dislike for small-town folk seems to run pretty deep. She doesn't seem the type to want to socialize with the lowly locals. It's surprising to see her here among the heathens. I wonder what she's up to."

"I'll find out," Pax said as he pushed his chair away from the table and stood. We looked at him in disbelief. "What?" He lifted his hands to his sides. "If she turned Eli down, then she clearly has some taste. Won't hurt to say hello."

"You're unbelievable; you know that?" I would have tossed his remaining beer at him, but nothing was worth wasting a free drink over.

Pax waggled his brows. "It's not every day a gorgeous woman comes through here. Especially one we haven't known since school … unless you're Owen, and you don't pay attention to the girls that were here from the beginning."

"Mean, but not untrue," Owen reasoned as he drank his cranberry and vodka. He glanced at Emily. "She's pretty."

"That's an understatement," Pax said. "She's Carl-level gorgeous."

"Is that your baseline standard for all women now?" I asked. "Because that makes it seem like you're still crushing on Owen's fiancée."

"It also means your standards are impossibly high because no one can reach the level of Carla," Owen added on.

Pax ignored us and walked over to the bar. We watched, seeing if he would fail. I wanted him to. Not necessarily because it was fun to see him flounder, but because I didn't want her to like him and loathe me.

We barely heard him introduce himself when she glanced at our table. I ducked my head down, but it was too late. She stared straight at me.

"I take it you're related to him?" Her tone hardened as her voice rose.

"Unfortunately, yes."

"I'm sorry. That must be awful for you."

Pax made a face as he ran a hand through his blond hair. "Aw, don't be like that. He's not that bad, but I promise I'm better. Are you going to judge me based on my brother?"

"Yes. You have a problem with that?"

"Doesn't seem particularly fair, or friendly, Miss Flanagan."

"Go back to your brothers and talk about football, or the snow, or something other than me."

I watched Pax cringe at the tone of her voice. "Kindness is free. Doesn't cost you a thing to smile or say a nice word."

"Do all the Cooper brothers talk first and think later? Or is it a Frazier Falls thing?"

Pax held up his hands in surrender. "Okay, I get it. You want to be left alone. There was no harm in seeing if you wanted to join us for a drink, though, was there?"

38

"You didn't make it far enough to ask."

"Nope, because your mouth opened first. Hope you have a better night."

She stood there with her jaw hanging open.

Paxton rejoined the table to bursts of laughter from both of us. "You deserved that," I said as he sat down looking like he'd walked through fire.

"She's got one hell of a sharp tongue on her."

"I can hear you, you know," Emily called from her place at the bar.

I looked up as she glanced at me. For the smallest of moments, the two of us almost smirked at each other, but then she looked away as John Reilly came out with a bag. I ignored my brothers and listened carefully to catch every word said.

"Here's the food for your mom," he said. "I've thrown in some of those dumplings she likes on the side. Tell her to hurry up and get better soon, okay?"

Emily gave him a warm smile, which transformed her already attractive face into something beautiful. "Thank you so much."

John looked toward our table. "Have you taken a liking to a Cooper?"

She laughed. "That's like asking me if I'd like a case of the pox."

John shook his head. "Mae West once said, 'Love thy neighbor, and if he happens to be tall, debonair, and devastating, it will be that much easier.' You could do a lot worse than a Cooper."

It was funny to hear John dish out his worldly words of wisdom to Emily. Lord, it was time he had a new audience.

"When they come up with a cure for stupidity, I'll consider it."

She gave me and my brothers a final look and left the bar.

It appeared she *could* be nice to small-town folk, or maybe only to John since he had food. Guess Miss Flanagan was more complicated than I'd originally thought.

"Hey, Eli, you want another?" Pax asked, holding up his empty mug. "Or are you going to sit there staring into space?"

"How can we already be on another round?" I'd been so focused on Emily that I missed everything around me.

Owen glanced at Pax's empty mug. "Somebody drank away his shame, and I drank with him in solidarity. You want another or not?"

I shook my head. "No, leave me out this time."

I wondered if I could find a reasonable excuse to visit Judy Flanagan's house. Emily was like an itch I couldn't reach. Maybe once I visited, she'd be out of my system for good.

Rich usually took wood from the mill to all the elderly residents in Frazier Falls. Between him and Pax, it was sometimes difficult to decide which one was saintlier. Maybe I needed to borrow the title for a day.

I supposed I could always call him and volunteer. At the thought, I froze. Why was I going to this much effort to see a woman I didn't like? Who or what was I becoming? *A damn masochist.*

Disappointed in myself, I downed my beer, then motioned over to Pax, who stood at the bar.

"I changed my mind. Grab me one while you're there."

Ridiculous thoughts about Emily should be easy to erase with copious amounts of alcohol.

CHAPTER SIX

EMILY

I wished my mom could eat spicy food. Meals were boring if I had to stick to mild and easy-to-digest ingredients. I craved garlic, and jalapeños, and hot sauce. God, I missed hot sauce. I was so damn sick of potatoes.

The massive sack that Eli's brother had found in the back of the store was a blessing, though there were only so many ways to make a potato. I wanted to burn all of them, simply so I didn't have to see them again, but I couldn't deny how versatile and filling they were. Besides, my mother loved them. I used to make fun of her for it, given that it made her look like an Irish stereotype. There was no potato famine in Frazier Falls.

"You worry too much about what people think of you, Emily," she had told me on more than one occasion. She was content to love her potatoes, be they mashed, or boiled, or roasted, or fried, and she didn't care how much I teased her about it.

There was no doubt I'd be a lot happier if I was more like my mother, but I couldn't be her because I was me. Opinionated. Cynical. Judgmental.

Eli's other brother, Paxton, was still grating on my nerves even now, two days after the fact. He had been so cocksure and arrogant like his brother. His easy charm wouldn't have been out of place in Los Angeles, but it seemed obnoxious in Frazier Falls. If I was being honest, had I met him in California, I would have had no qualms about going home with him after a night of drinking and dancing.

The problem was, he wasn't from California. He was from Frazier Falls, Colorado, and no different from his brother. Full of himself in a way only a man who knew everything about the people and places around him could be, but I wasn't going to give him an opportunity to get to know me. I'd remain a mystery and forget the Coopers existed once I went home.

The other brother, Owen, was the engaged one, I assumed. Beyond frustrated, it annoyed every cell in my body that their names had stuck in my head after Sadie had shared her social media search. Out of the three brothers, he was the one who seemed the most level-headed and normal.

Technically, there was nothing bad about Eli or Paxton. Paxton had relented quickly when it became obvious I wanted him to leave me alone, and Eli had helped me with the potatoes I now peeled. He'd held the door open for me—though I was fairly certain he'd only done it to prove a point. Then again, he'd saved me from falling, which he didn't have to do.

It was all well and good to say that I'd forget about him and his brothers when I returned to Los Angeles, but I was still in Frazier Falls, which meant running into Eli was a likely scenario. I'd now seen him twice in as many days. It was a miracle I hadn't seen him before.

Looking out the kitchen window, the noonday sun shone as strongly as it could in the middle of winter, reflecting brilliantly off the snow. If it stayed like this over the next couple of days, then flights would resume in and out of the smaller airports. I could realistically be out of here by Wednesday.

I peeked at my mom through the open door. She was sitting on the sofa, wrapped in a blanket, watching old episodes of Downton Abbey. She always found something British to keep her occupied. Shaking my head in bemusement, I returned to cooking her lunch.

"That smells delicious," she said in anticipation as I placed our food on the small dining table.

"Meat and potatoes would taste much better if you'd let me spice up the seasoning."

"Don't be ridiculous. You can't go wrong with the classics. Leave them be."

I grabbed the pepper mill and twisted it until a cloud of black dust covered my meat. It was my version of blackened steak. "As long as you're happy with it."

"I'm delighted to have someone cooking for me. You know how much I appreciate it, right?"

"Yes, I do." I glanced out of the window once more.

"Why don't you head on out after lunch and explore a bit? The woods here are beautiful."

"The snow is still too thick on the ground for me to take you out."

She fussed in exasperation. "By yourself, I mean. It's about time you used your eyes and ears and took in a bit of the place you're actually in rather than daydreaming about where you'd rather be. Thinking about that city of yours won't make the snow melt any faster. Slow down and enjoy this while you can."

I narrowed my eyes at her, feeling the crease from the tension in my forehead. "Is this an order?"

"If it'll get you outside, then yes, it's an order. Get out of the house. Don't come back until sunset. Go wandering through the trees and visit the creek. It must be frozen solid right now. I'm sure it's beautiful. Take some photos on your phone for your poor old mother to see."

I let out a huff. "Fine." I sounded like a sulky teenager. "I'll go outside. Though I'm sure to hate every moment of it to spite you." I looked up with a smile.

She smiled back. "That's the spirit."

Resigned to my fate, I finished my lunch and threw on as many layers as I thought I'd need. I twisted my hair into a bun, sighing at the flyways I could never control. Forgoing a hat in favor of a pair of fluffy earmuffs, I slid on a pair of leather gloves before waving goodbye to my mother.

"If the weather stays like this, you'll be back to yourself in no time," I murmured as I stepped outside. That was my hope. My mom would no doubt enjoy getting out of the house, and it would lessen the blow of my departure.

My heart still hurt at the thought of her staying here by herself. There was no guarantee the weather was going to keep getting better until spring. Today's good weather could merely be a blip. Long enough for me to get the hell out of here, but not long enough to allow her to get better. What else could I do?

As I walked, I passed lots of houses with well-built, wooden porches covered in a layer of snow. I made my way out of town toward the edge of the forest. The houses became more spread out with large areas of parkland in between. There was a children's jungle gym covered in more snow than I would have thought physically possible. The sounds of kids laughing filled the air as they happily flung themselves down a hill on everything from a cardboard box to a trash can lid.

Snow to a child was magical. I'd never gotten much of it in Ireland, where it was often too wet and mild, but there had been one or two occasions when we'd been the recipient of a snow-storm. The aftereffects had been nothing like the snow in Frazier

Falls, but there had been enough snow for sledding. Enough to build a snowman. Enough to have fun. But I was no longer a child. I was an adult out for a walk imposed on me as some brutal form of punishment from my mother. Maybe I was still a child, after all.

The shrieks of delight from the children disappeared as I reached the line of trees that signaled the beginning of the forest. Here, by the park, many of the trees were deciduous, their naked branches waiting for winter to end. Up ahead, the forest gave way to all kinds of coniferous trees, and the mill I'd spied on more than one occasion when traveling through to visit my mom.

There was spruce and fir and pine. Possibly more. I'd never been much of a tree person, but given my background in geography, it came as a surprise to no one that I knew more than the average person about the world around me.

After walking beneath the snow-heavy boughs melting under the rays of sunlight, I had to admit my mom had been right. Getting out was good. It was beautiful here. Quiet and peaceful with air as crisp and clean as freshly pressed linen.

It was the perfect place for my mom to be even if I didn't want to admit it. My lungs felt like they were being cleansed simply by breathing in the air. Air like this didn't exist in Los Angeles. Sadly, it reminded me of home.

My laughter echoed through the trees. Ardmore hadn't been my home in eighteen years. I'd spent more time in Los Angeles than in Ireland, and yet, despite all that, when I thought of home, I always thought of that tiny, inconsequential village in the middle of nowhere.

Eventually, after a bit of an uphill climb following the footsteps of someone who had broken a trail before me, I broke through the tree line and found myself in a narrow clearing at the top of a hill. I could see the entire town below me.

An unexpected "wow" escaped my lips as I took in the sight.

The sun shone on a frozen ribbon that must have been the creek, the glinting rays turning it to silver.

Sitting beneath a tree on the snow-packed ground, I closed my eyes and took in the sounds of chirping birds and rustling pine needles as the wind skated through the forest. I'd never admit this to anyone, but this moment was perfect.

CHAPTER SEVEN

ELI

Despite having told myself I wouldn't ask my future brother-in-law to help with his firewood deliveries, I said yes to his request to do the rounds of the forest. He had this obsession to make sure it was free of litter. He policed it like a ranger. Given that he and my brother were in Germany, it was hard to say no.

On a Sunday, I would have rather stayed in and had a few beers with Paxton, but I found myself in the woods. Now that the weather had cleared up, and the warmth of the sun enticed me outside, I had to admit that I was enjoying it.

Doing the rounds was more time consuming during the summer, when teenagers would often use it as their drinking and camping grounds, but now, in the dead of winter, there wasn't a person around. Having nothing to clean on the outskirts led me to believe the inner forest would be completely fine. I was half-tempted to call it a day, but something kept me pressing forward. It was probably the sun at my back.

With the snow lying thick on the ground, it was impossible to use the roads through the woods. Even the Cooper Construction truck with its snow tires and four-wheel-drive struggled, so I was forced to park by the side of the road once I couldn't move forward.

"On foot I go, then," I murmured, the words coming out as cloudy puffs of breath in the freezing air.

It was beautiful in the forest, the mid-afternoon sunlight shining a path through the undergrowth for me to follow. As the pines grew thicker and taller and I moved deeper, less light filtered down to the undergrowth. Eventually, I was walking through a murky, silent twilight, the air free of the chattering of birds, the slight breeze no longer moving the needles. The canopy was so dense that little snow had hit the ground.

Breathing became harder as the path sloped upward, signaling the beginning of the hill where the oldest trees grew. I hadn't been up the hill for several years since the trees at the top were never felled. They towered above the forest canopy—tall sentries looking over the town for all of time and eternity.

I imagined being one of those trees, whiling away your life watching the goings-on of Frazier Falls and never knowing that there are far more interesting places to be.

I chuckled at the thought. That job would be a dream for me. Watching. Listening.

"Except I'm not a tree, and I do enjoy a good fire, which would be cannibalistic if I were a tree," I said aloud, shocked by the echo that returned to haunt me as I passed through a rare clearing in the forest. The sunlight painted the area in silver and gold, the snow on the rocks glistening in a futile attempt to melt before the darkness of night set in.

I brushed the snow from one of the rocks and sat down to take in the surrounding sights. All the clearing needed was an errant deer rummaging around for a stray patch of grass, and the image of a winter paradise would be complete. While I remained sitting here, a deer, or any other animal for that matter, would never dare show its face for fear of becoming dinner. Sighing, I got up and moved on, continuing my steady, twisting climb up the hill.

Eventually, it got to the point where I had to admit that I was bored, and without the sun, my walk underneath the trees had grown cold. I rubbed my hands together, my gloves doing nothing to heat me.

I had to come back down once I reached the top. I knew I should call it quits and leave before numbness set in, and yet, I didn't. I must have walked at least three-quarters of the way up the hill. There were another ten minutes to go before I reached the top. Another ten minutes to freeze. I fumbled for my cell phone to check the time—it was past four. The sun would be low in the sky, painting the entire town in sunset tones of gold and red and purple. The view from the top of the hill would be worth the discomfort.

I plowed through the snow, ignoring my numb, stinging fingers, and the vague ache in my calf muscles until the trees thinned and the steep, uphill incline smoothed out. When I reached the last of the trees, I heard a noise I hadn't been expecting —a voice.

What was someone doing all the way up here? They must be as crazy as me. The irony of the situation was not lost. Something caused me to retreat behind a pine tree, keeping me concealed, while I worked out who it was that was up here on their own.

"He'll help you with the potatoes that you're so obviously looking for," the voice said rather sarcastically. It was female and familiar … and Irish.

"Oh, no, she hasn't told me her name; I must bribe it out of her." Emily continued, in a sing-song voice as if she were recounting a fairytale to a young child. "Save me from hitting my head, my arse. He was the reason I fell in the first place."

Okay, that bit wasn't part of any fairytale I'd ever heard before.

Even bad language sounded wonderful in Emily Flanagan's accent. I was certain I could listen to her insult me all day and still crave more.

"But what the hell is she doing …?" I wondered quietly but aloud.

"Then that woman—Lucy—the one who 'helps' my ma sometimes!" she exclaimed. "What is she after? Is she trying to weasel her way into the will? Ma has nothing. Lucy could have it. Nothing is nothing, no matter how much you divide it up."

"Hey, that's not fair," I protested out loud. I heard Emily gasp as she took in the fact that she wasn't alone.

"Who's there?" she called out, uncertainty painting her voice.

"You're going to hate that it's me," I admitted, not moving from my position of relative safety behind a tree.

"That's you, Eli, isn't it?"

"In the flesh."

I could practically see Emily's eyes narrowing in suspicion even from where I was standing.

"Did you follow me all the way up here?"

"Lord no. I was doing the rounds."

"You were doing the—for God's sake, stop hiding behind a tree, and face me like a grown man."

I bowed my head beneath a branch as I made my way out of the tree line and into the glorious sunshine and the most outstanding view of Frazier Falls one could get.

I swung around with a hand protecting my eyes from the glare of the sun, looking for Emily. I found her sitting beneath the canopy of trees several yards away from the one I'd been hiding behind.

I gave her a broad smile. "Hardly believe you made it all the way up here, given how much you hate the town."

She rolled her eyes. "Ma wanted me to go for a walk."

"You were kicked out? At your age?"

"What of it?" Emily fired back defensively.

I shrugged. "Nothing much. It's just funny."

"What did you mean by doing the rounds?"

"I was making sure nobody had messed up part of the forest. With Rich gone, I took over his searching for unattended camp-fires or trash left by teenagers or idiots."

Emily frowned. "Seems a bit cold for that, even for underage drinkers."

"I know, but the rounds still have to be done. Rich and Owen flew out this morning for Germany. Pax is helping out in Wilkes' again, so that left me." I threw my arms in the air in a mock cele-bration. "Hooray."

"You ... do you own the forest?"

I nodded as I made my way over to sit down beside her. Emily immediately backed away.

"What the hell do you think you're doing?"

I looked at her pointedly. "Sitting down. It's freezing out. I could do with proximal body heat, and so could you."

She looked as if she desperately wanted to argue, but after a moment or two, she gave up.

"Fine. Do what you like," She looked at me quizzically. "Do you own the whole forest?"

"No, my brothers and I only own the southern part—the area closer to the creek. The Stevensons own the rest. They're the siblings who run the mill."

"That basically means your family owns the whole forest now."

I frowned. "What do you mean?"

"Because Carla is marrying—oh. Shite."

I put two and two together halfway through Emily's sentence. I almost laughed in response.

"Have you been stalking me, Miss Flanagan?"

"Not you, but your family. It was my friend from California, not me."

"And how did your friend know to investigate a family she's never met in a town she's never been to?"

Emily looked away, a red flush pinking her cheeks. Or at least, she might have been blushing. Her face had been so red with the cold already; it was hard to tell.

"I may have been trash talking about you to her. She looked you up."

"What? Then she recited my entire family history for your benefit?"

She winced. "Would you believe me if I said it was pretty much exactly like that?"

"Strangely enough, yes. Something tells me your stubborn pride wouldn't let you so much as type my name into a computer no matter how curious you were."

"I don't know whether that's a compliment or an insult."

I glanced at her and was momentarily distracted by the sunlight glinting off her beautiful green eyes. Her hair was reflecting it, too, setting it on fire. Emily Flanagan was stunning. Even I was man enough to admit that.

"Let's call it a bit of both."

"Wonderful."

The two of us were silent for a few minutes, Emily not looking at me as I busied myself with watching the town below us.

As I followed the silvery ribbon of the frozen creek with my eyes, Emily broke the silence.

"What did you mean that I wasn't being fair?"

"Huh?"

"When you broke your cover in the trees," she said, pointing back to where I'd been hidden. "I was talking about Lucy Rogers—"

"You mean you were bitching about Lucy Rogers."

"Point taken. What did you mean?" She picked at the stray pine needles peeking through the snow.

"I meant exactly what I said. You weren't being fair. Sure, Lucy's a busybody and probably the nosiest person in the town, but she's a good person. She gets along with your mom. Her daughter Rose must be close to your age. They probably talk about the two of you to one another. How old are you, anyway—thirty? Thirty-two?"

"I'm thirty-three. I didn't know they actually got on that well…"

"Then maybe you should pay attention to the people who are looking out for your mom."

Emily's nose wrinkled in annoyance at the comment, but then she sighed.

"You're right. Want a medal?"

"You got one? I look good in gold." I laughed, shifting against the tree to make myself more comfortable. My arm ended up accidentally brushing up against Emily's, but she didn't pull away.

"Your impersonation of me was pretty spot-on, though," I admitted.

Emily backed away slightly in horror. "Oh, Lord. You heard that part, too?"

"That was the whole reason I hid. So, tell me, who else can you do?"

Emily frowned uncertainly. "What do you mean?"

"The people in town. Who else do you think you've got pegged? Give me the run-down, and I'll tell you if you're right or not."

"That sounds … pretty mean. And judgmental."

"That's exactly the point." I gave her a look that told her I knew who she was. Like it or not, she was like me, and somehow that made her being in Frazier Falls perfect.

CHAPTER EIGHT

EMILY

Of all the things to be doing in the world, I never thought I'd be sitting up on the top of a hill imitating the people down below in Frazier Falls with Eli Cooper.

"You seriously want me to tell you what I think of the people in town?"

Eli nodded. "Absolutely."

Something told me that Eli wouldn't leave until I did, and I had to admit that our conversation had been the first one I'd enjoyed with anyone other than my mom or Sadie in weeks.

"Okay. Who should I start with?"

"Have you met Rachel Wilkes?"

"What, you mean the ancient lady who runs the convenience store when she doesn't have Paxton take over for her?"

"That's the one. Though she's not that old. I'm pretty sure she's a couple years younger than your mom."

"No way!" That information came as a shock. "I could have sworn she was older, and that's not to mention that my mom doesn't exactly look like a young seventy, either."

"Some people are simply cursed with bad genes, I guess."

"But not you, right?" I said with a smirk. "You and your brothers are absolutely perfect."

"Hey, you've already roasted me. Do Rachel."

"I don't have much to say about her, except I'm pretty sure she has no clue how to run a shop."

"Exactly, right?" Eli replied with surprising excitement. "There's no way her age has anything to do with it. She doesn't know how to actually stock shelves or work a register, and now it's too late to ask someone to teach her."

I burst out laughing. "You know, that's exactly right. I've been in a few times over the years when I've flown in to see my mom, and she has never known where the canned tomatoes are even though I make a point of asking every time I'm in."

"Sounds about right. Hey, if you've visited here so often, how come I've never seen you?"

"It's not as if I stay long." I grimaced at the thought of staying in Frazier Falls. "I'm only ever here to see my mom, so generally, I stay with her. My visits are usually a day or two over the weekends. It's not all that surprising that you haven't seen me. We spend our time sitting in the living room catching up."

"I suppose … okay, next one. Have you met Brady Huck?"

"Ugh, is he the guy who runs that other bar? The one down the street from Reilly's?"

"That would be the one. Doesn't sound like you hold him in high regard."

I rolled my eyes. "He hit on me a couple years back when my mom insisted on taking me to Huck's for a drink. The man told me I reminded him of Hermione Granger because of my accent. What a dullard. She's British. Not even close. The guy's a real creep."

"I'm fairly certain he's a creep to everyone, and that's a valid reason to dislike him."

"He seems like the kind of guy who might piss on his neighbor's daisies."

Eli almost choked in response. "Definitely guilty of that, except they were roses. He said it was an emergency and couldn't make it the extra twenty feet indoors."

"Yuck. Why does anyone go to his bar if he's such a creep?"

"Because his dad's a decent man, and the place is cheaper than Reilly's. Also, you'll never get kicked out, which is a plus."

I raised an eyebrow. "You have cause to take that as a plus?"

"Owen got us kicked out of Reilly's a couple times." Eli chuckled. "Once for fist-fighting with Rich, and once, for over two weeks, for being an asshole to Ruthie McCall on a date."

"Is that the barmaid who's always on her phone?"

"Only recently. She's met a guy in the next town over … hopefully, he's less of a dick than my brother."

I frowned. "I had Owen pegged as the nice one out of you Coopers."

"Not Pax?"

"He doesn't count. He's almost too nice. There must be something going on with him behind the scenes."

"For a girl who doesn't like this town, you sure have your finger on the pulse. You're good at this. Owen usually is the nice one, but he was a bit of an accidental playboy before he met Carla."

"How can one be an accidental playboy?"

"It's possible if you're never aware that's what you are," Eli replied. "That, and Owen is pretty charming and can't say no. That's a bad combination when it comes to women asking him out."

"I suppose. What's Paxton's deal?"

"Basically," Eli shrugged his shoulders, "he's actually great with people. They tell him everything he needs to know before realizing he's wormed the information out of them for a reason."

"He doesn't look like you or Owen." I turned to look at Eli. The scruff on his face called out to me to touch it to see if it was soft, but it was too cold to remove my gloves to find out. "Was he from a different marriage or adopted?"

"Nope, he's one hundred percent our brother by blood," Eli smirked. "Though we made damn sure to try to convince him he was adopted when he was a kid."

"That's cruel."

"That should be right up your alley."

I couldn't help but laugh. "I'm not terrible all the time, you know. I can be nice."

"I know. You're being nice now."

"I'm literally making fun of everyone in Frazier Falls."

"Yes, but you're doing it because I asked you to, and I'm joining in."

"That doesn't make me nice. That makes us both terrible people."

Eli stared at the tiny, twinkling town down below. The sun was setting lower and lower in the sky, causing everything to sparkle as if it were made of diamonds instead of brick and lumber.

"I suppose you're right," he murmured.

The comment took me aback with its sincerity.

"I had half-expected you to vehemently deny that," I admitted. "Who confesses to being a bad person?"

He looked at me, and part of my brain confirmed that his eyes were indeed blue—like a summer sky, rather than a winter one. They were beautiful. It occurred to me that Eli was way too close to me, but something prevented me from moving away.

"I don't believe either of us are truly bad people," Eli said, his voice low. "We're a little on the critical side. Nothing wrong with that."

"Clearly, there is. If I can't even thank a person for stopping me from falling flat on my face out of spite, and you can't go shopping without deliberately pissing off a stranger, we might have to consider the possibility that we're not nice."

"I'm nice, and you're nice." He winked. "I bet we'd be nice together."

"Have you been talking to my friend, Sadie?"

"No, but would she tell me your secrets?"

"I don't have secrets." *I wanted to lean forward and kiss him.* But that was a secret I'd never tell.

He laughed. "We all have secrets."

I leaned back and arched a brow. "Tell me yours, Mr. Cooper."

He scooted closer, rubbing his shoulder against mine and despite the cold temps, a rush of heat flowed through my body.

"I'm a closet Cosmopolitan reader."

I gasped. "No way. Why?"

"Women read it," he said matter of fact like. "It gives me an edge against the less educated men."

"Not sure that's true, but okay, what else?"

"There's a picture out there somewhere of me wearing a thong."

I laughed. "Women's or men's?"

"Not sure. In all fairness, there was a lot of whiskey and a dare involved."

"So, you have problems with impulse control."

"I do," He leaned forward until his lips were so close, I could feel the warmth of his breath. "I've got terrible self-control."

Nothing could have prepared me for Eli's response. He pressed his lips against mine, and he kissed me. Before I knew what was going on, or how it had transpired, I was kissing him back.

Here, on the top of a snow-covered hill overlooking what was for some people, their entire world, Eli and I indulged in an immediate attraction we hadn't wanted to admit to anyone, even ourselves.

His lips were hot and wet against my own—a welcome heat against the cold pressing in around us. I leaned in closer, allowing Eli to slide a gloved hand behind the nape of my neck even though it was frozen. It felt like hours had passed before we finally broke away.

Eli grinned foolishly. "Kind of feels like we've snuck behind the bleachers during a football game to make out like high schoolers," he joked.

"You do that kind of thing often, Cooper?" He was probably a playboy like his older brother, Owen, but this wasn't accidental. I imagined Eli did everything with a purpose.

He shook his head. "Maybe back in the day."

But the moment was abruptly interrupted by a dark shadow overcoming us. Eli glanced up, cursing.

"What's wrong—oh, Lord no," I bit out, making a noise of exasperation as I noticed the dark, murky clouds rolling in over the forest directly behind us. "Just my luck. They're going to close the airport again, aren't they?"

"By the look of those clouds, I'm afraid so. Owen and Rich are going to get stranded too."

I wasn't concerned about Owen or Rich. If the storm rolled in, I was good and stuck again. Resigned to my fate, I asked, "Germany isn't a bad place to be stuck, is it?"

"They'll probably be fine on the international flight, but they'll likely get stranded in New York."

"Oh no, that's awful," I responded in as dry and flat a voice as possible.

Eli laughed, shaking his head. "Might sound great to you, but Owen has some bad experiences associated with the city."

"Okay, now I'm intrigued. And here I was thinking you guys never left Frazier Falls."

"Excuse you, Miss Flanagan, but all three of us Cooper brothers are college-educated. I'll have you know; I studied accounting and finance at Northeastern."

"No way."

"I did, I swear."

I shook my head in doubt. "I'm going to have to see your diploma to believe it."

"That could be arranged." There was a spark of indefinable emotion in his eyes. Not knowing him well enough, I couldn't tell if it was humor or passion.

I clung to that thought. Could he want more than a stolen kiss? I wasn't sure, so I kept the conversation active.

"And what about your brothers? Where did they study?"

"Do I get to ask you where you studied?"

"You can. Doesn't mean I'll answer."

"Of course not."

The winter sky hung heavy above us, spitting the beginnings of dime-size snowflakes in our direction.

"A conversation for another time," Eli said, catching the expression on my face. He got up to his feet. "Come on. We should get back down to civilization before this storm lets loose."

I nodded in agreement as I struggled to my feet, my muscles were cramped and sore from sitting in the same position for so long. Eli held out a hand to help steady me, which, to my own surprise, I took.

"Thank you," I said, which shocked him as much as it did me.

"I wasn't aware you knew how to say those words with sincerity. That's twice today," he joked.

"Haha, you're hilarious." I looked around, searching for an escape. "Do you know the fastest way out of the forest?"

He pointed down the hill. "You basically head toward town and run as fast as you can."

I gave him an unamused, level stare, which Eli merely laughed at.

"Follow me."

Forty minutes later, we had made our way down the hill, and as we headed farther out of the forest, the trees began to change from pine trees to barren sticks, showing us more and more of the brooding gray sky as a result.

When I headed in the general direction of my mom's house, Eli grabbed my arm and nodded in the opposite way.

"I have a truck. Let me drive you."

"Are you sure?" I asked, uncertain. "It looks like the snow's going to come down in blankets any moment now. If you take me home first, the roads might be too bad for you to get back yourself."

"A risk I'll have to take in my role as a gentleman."

"So, you're playing at being a gentleman?"

"No, but I'm not letting you walk back. I've seen how unbalanced you are on the ice."

"That was your fault, and you know it," I complained as we rushed in the direction of his truck. The snow fell heavier, filtering down between the empty branches of the trees. The big flakes melted against our skin, stinging our faces with icy coldness.

"Surely a ride home makes up for it?" he reasoned as we reached the truck. Frozen shut, it took Eli a few tries to open the passenger door. The interior was bitterly cold, but he hiked up the heat as soon as he started the engine.

"If you get me home in one piece, then we'll call it even," I watched through a half fogged-up window as Eli reversed down the forest road until he could turn the truck around. With every jostle and bump, I worried that he'd burst a tire or damage the truck to the point that we'd be stuck here, but eventually, we cleared the forest road.

By then, the snow fell, so heavy and thick, we could barely see.

"Are you sure you're going to get home okay?" I asked when we pulled in front of my mom's house.

"Careful, Flanagan, that almost sounds like you care."

"And smart-ass Eli is back."

"Give me your number, and I'll text you when I get home, so you don't worry."

I was tempted to refuse, simply for the way he worded his request, but eventually, genuine concern overrode my need to insult him. I recited my number while Eli punched it into his phone, then felt my own phone vibrate a few seconds later.

"I've texted you, so you have my number, too," he said.

"No, you were checking to make sure I didn't give you a fake number." Our conversation on the hill was invigorating, or maybe that was the snow, but then there was the kiss ... yes, the kiss was a surprise. A nice surprise. Sadie would eat every detail of it up, but I was keeping this one to myself.

He looked out his window into the blizzard that seemed to be hovering over his truck. "Given the weather, it would seem that you might be around for a while longer."

I made a face. "I was supposed to leave by Wednesday."

"Guess that's good for me. And it gives you more time with your mom."

That was the only plus. "That's true." I waved him off and climbed out of the truck.

I resisted the urge to look back as I made my way up the path to the front door, but when I reached it, I glanced behind me and saw that Eli hadn't moved.

He rolled down the window. "Had to make sure you didn't fall on your face," he called out, laughing to himself as he drove away.

I gave him the finger in response, though I knew he wouldn't be able to see it.

Inside the house, my mom was curled up on the sofa in the gloriously warm living room. She looked at me and smiled.

"Did you have a nice time, sweetheart?"

"Yes." I brought my fingers to my lips. "A really nice time." The puffiness and tingly feeling still lingered there, but it had nothing to do with the cold.

CHAPTER NINE

ELI

With the snow coming down hard and fast once more, I couldn't help but think of Emily, and how her hopes of getting out of Frazier Falls were now crushed. It was Thursday, and the weather showed no signs of letting up.

Owen and Rich were stranded in New York just as I had predicted, which meant Carla was in a thoroughly bad mood. She'd been staying at Owen's place. I had to wonder why she hadn't moved in permanently, given that they were engaged. In Owen's absence, Pax and I had come around to keep her company.

"They're out of hot chocolate." She stomped her foot. "Wilkes' is out of hot chocolate, and I'm going mad."

"Carla, are you sure someone isn't accidentally spiking your hot chocolate with something stronger? You sound like you're going through withdrawal."

"Hilarious, Eli."

"I suppose sugar can be as addictive—though it sounds particularly less badass to say you're addicted to sugar."

She fisted her hands on her hips. "Tell me, why didn't you

pursue a career in stand-up comedy? Clearly, you missed your calling."

"I know you meant that as an insult, but I'm going to take it at face value, and thank you for the compliment." I ducked out of the way when Carla threw a sofa cushion at my head.

"You're impossible."

"You know, Carl," Pax said from his position in the corner chair, "I might have some cocoa powder at my house. I'll have a look tonight and bring it over in the morning if I do."

Carla's eyes lit up. "Really?" The corners of her lips tilted into a smile." I always knew I liked you best."

"Don't get your hopes up. He's not going back to his place." I moved closer to the fireplace, soaking up the heat. "If you think he's going anywhere other than the spare room tonight, then you're sorely mistaken."

Pax grumbled. He was trying and failing to read. I had to wonder why he would attempt such a solitary venture in the presence of Carla and me.

He made a face. "You have no faith in me."

"I've seen you drive in the snow. It's not pretty." I said, smirking. "But your crush on Carla might—"

"Stop being an ass," Pax complained, rolling over to face the fire. We knew his pouting would last all of five minutes … less if I cracked open a beer for him, which is what I did. He sat up and grabbed it from me in a second. "I take it back. You're only an ass sometimes."

"It's a brother's duty to make his sibling's life as annoying as possible—something which you're rather adept at," I said, laughing when he scowled.

"I'll let that one slide, but only because you gave me a beer."

"You're easy to bribe."

"Maybe I know when to quit."

66

"Like with Emily the other night?" I threw out.

"Oh? What's this?" Carla asked curiously. "Where's my beer, Eli? It sounds like the entertainment is just beginning."

"I thought you and Owen weren't drinking beer anymore."

"That's only Owen. He says it makes him bloated." Carla laughed. "I'm still happy to drink it. Besides, those are my beers you're handing out."

"I knew you were a generous host." Feeling the heat start to singe my skin, I moved away from the fire. "I'll replace them," I headed back to the refrigerator to get her a beer.

"You won't have to if you tell me what went down."

"Fair enough." I handed her a bottle.

She returned her gaze to Paxton. "What happened with this woman you were talking about? Elaine?"

"Emily," I corrected without thinking. Carla glanced at me but looked back at Pax.

He let out an exaggerated sigh. "What can I say? I gave it a shot, and she completely rejected me. I'm man enough to accept that."

"She destroyed you, that's what she did," I said, smirking.

"Fine. Truth is, she didn't even give me time to take a shot. Though that's hardly worse than Eli arguing with her in a convenience store, and then making her fall flat on her ass."

Carla nearly spat out her beer in laughter. "What? That doesn't sound like you at all, Eli." She had perfected her sarcastic tone. It wasn't nearly as good as Emily's, but she had promise.

"Very funny," I muttered. "I'm over it. Besides, Emily's not bad. She's actually likable."

That piqued Pax's attention.

"When did you see her again?"

I grimaced. I didn't want to talk about her to my brother. I didn't even know where I stood on the matter of how I felt about her, so what was I supposed to say?

"I met her on Sunday when the weather was better," I ended up saying. "She was out for a walk. We talked for a bit and cleared the air, so to speak. When the weather got worse, I drove her back to her mom's place."

Pax frowned. "But you were in the forest on Sunday, covering for Rich."

"Which was where I found her having a walk."

"The two of you were alone, in the forest, all afternoon?" Pax grinned mischievously.

"I know exactly what you're insinuating, and I can tell you … it's only slightly like that."

"Oh?" Carla let out. "Now, you definitely have my interest." She leaned into the corner of the big leather sofa and pulled a crocheted blanket over her lap. She was in for the long haul.

I didn't even know why I told them the truth. Maybe I was trying to work things out myself by speaking out loud.

"We may have kissed, but that was it. The weather was turning, so we had—"

"Would you have gone further if the snow wasn't against you?" Pax asked.

"In what world would you willingly get any more naked than you had to be in freezing temperatures?"

"I wouldn't," Pax snapped back. "But, I'm not impulsive."

"You're a Cooper, which means you often act without thought." I tipped back my beer for a deep drink. "Even if a storm hadn't been blowing in, it was far too cold to do 'anything else,' and you know it."

"Point taken, buzzkill," Pax huffed out an exasperated breath. "Only you could make gossip so boring."

"It's not gossip if it's about me, and I'm the one telling you about it."

"You get what I mean. Anyway, are you going to see her again?"

I paused. In all honesty, I didn't know.

"I guess the weather will determine that," I said. "I mean, she wants to leave as soon as the snow lets up. I might see her again if it stays bad."

"Now the weather is working for you? That's a fun turn of events."

As I was about to push back at Paxton, all the lights flickered in the house.

I glanced at Carla. "The backup generator is in good shape, right?"

She nodded. "Owen checked it before he left. If the power goes out, it'll come back on."

Half an hour later, Carla's statement proved to be correct. The power cut out, and a few seconds after, the generator kicked into gear, and the house was lit again.

"I wonder how long we'll be without power," Paxton mused. "I installed new generators in Rachel Wilkes' and Lucy's houses—"

"Why Lucy? Her previous generator was completely fine." He chuckled. "She wanted an excuse for you to come around, right?"

"She's a sweetheart, and don't give me a hard time for worrying about the older residents."

"How many of them will be without power?" I asked.

Pax shrugged. "Some of them, for sure. Not all of these old houses have been updated yet. To be honest, the sooner they all get behind Owen's Green House Project, the better."

"You'd think the massive discounts we're giving would be enough to shift them into gear," Carla grumbled. "Owen's offering it at cost."

"You can bet your ass you'll get a ton of new orders once this weather has passed. Nobody wants to be caught in a situation where their house can't handle this kind of weather again." It was then that it struck me.

"Pax, do you know if Judy Flanagan's house has a backup generator?"

He laughed. "You're trying to find a way to see Emily again, aren't you?"

"Shut up. I'm serious. You know Judy's health is terrible, and she can't afford to have the power out."

"God knows a city girl like Emily isn't likely to be able to make a fire to save her life," Pax said.

"Paxton," I warned.

He held up his hands in surrender. "You were the one who said she was an insufferable city girl. When was the last time you met someone from the city who could build a good fire?"

"You're right," I had to admit. "Back to the question. Do you know if Judy's house has a generator?"

He shook his head. "I don't think so. Her house is old, even by Frazier Falls standards. I think the chances of her having one are slim."

"That's all I needed to know." I put my bottle on the table and grabbed my jacket before heading for the door.

"Eli, you can't seriously be heading over there in this weather," Carla called after me. "You could get hurt."

"The Flanagan's will be worse off if they don't have heat. I'm going to take some of Owen's firewood. I'll replace it later."

"No, you won't," Carla called out as I slammed the door shut behind me.

"Yeah, you're right, I definitely won't," I said out loud right before I grabbed armfuls of wood and headed to my truck. I started the engine and drove straight toward Judy's house ... and Emily.

Time to teach the city girl how to build a fire.

CHAPTER TEN

EMILY

I resisted the urge to flinch when the lightbulb in my bedroom flickered. It had been doing that on and off for the past three hours, as had the rest of the lights in my mother's house. I knew what it meant. The power was doomed to fail sooner rather than later.

To my disappointment, it happened sooner. I should have plugged my laptop in to charge hours ago.

The whole house went dark and eerily quiet all at once. The comforting, ever-present noises associated with the heater, the oxygen tank, and the television, were gone in an instant.

I looked at my laptop. It had five percent battery left.

"Just my luck ..." I grumbled.

I'd been stuck in Frazier Falls because of the new storm, and it forced me to pick up work from Sadie that I could complete remotely. I knew I had to get back by Monday. Our February projects depended on it, but that didn't seem likely after checking the weather forecast. Nothing was due to improve until at least the middle of next week.

As a geographer and a failed-wannabe-meteorologist, I knew how difficult it was to make accurate long-term weather forecasts. The current one could be completely wrong, and the tumultuous front that was tormenting Colorado might be gone by the weekend. On the other hand, it could stay far longer than forecasted.

I sighed heavily. There was no use brooding in a dark room. I had to find candles and flashlights and set up a fire.

When I padded downstairs, I found my mother on the sofa, snoozing. The imminent cold would wake her soon. It would fill her lungs and make it difficult to breathe. I only had a limited time to get a fire going before the cold woke her. The biggest problem I faced was we were out of wood.

"How did this happen?" I complained under my breath, furious. Upon reflection, I had no one to blame but myself. Since I'd discovered a new love of building long-burning fires, the fireplace barely saw a day without one. It was no wonder we had run out.

I hurried to locate the stash of candles my mom kept, strategically placing them around the house to light up the rooms. Then I found a flashlight and struggled outside to the shed in the hopes of finding more wood, but the roof of the shed was leaking, and the wood inside was either wet, frozen, or rotted to the core.

"What do I do now?" I worried, knowing that Wilkes' would certainly be closed, not to mention they were probably out of firewood, too. "If only Ma had gotten a bloody backup generator installed," I muttered as I made my way back inside. That was confirmation that I needed to keep working in Los Angeles. The pay was good and allowed me to provide the things mom's small retirement check couldn't.

When I moved through the living room, I felt the marked drop in temperature from ten minutes prior. If I didn't get the fire up and running soon, or if the power didn't come back on in the next hour or so, the house would end up as icy as an igloo.

I ran upstairs and took several blankets from the hallway closet and rushed back to the living room with them. I covered my mom as I checked her oxygen tank for good measure. No electricity meant no oxygen. She barely stirred, which only worried me more.

As I started to panic, a knock rattled the door. Odd, I thought. Who in the world would come knocking in this weather? Then I felt a buzzing in my pocket, so I pulled out my phone to find a text from Eli.

Open the damn door. I come bearing gifts.

I rushed over immediately to let him in. He stood there with an armful of firewood. I almost kissed him on the spot.

"How did you know?" I asked breathlessly as I closed the door behind him. "Our firewood ran out."

"Pax was pretty sure your mom didn't have a backup generator, so I took a guess that you guys may be in trouble. With you being a city gal with no fire-making skills and all, I rushed like a knight ready to rescue." He moved to the cold fireplace and stacked on the wood.

"I'll have you know," I said as he took off his jacket, "that I'm pretty damn good at making fires."

He threw me a look. "Hard to believe, Flanagan."

"Okay, I didn't know how to build one until a few days ago, but that was nothing a quick internet search couldn't fix."

He laughed. "And yet you ended up running out of firewood in the middle of a storm. Sounds like you've got everything covered." He grabbed his jacket. "Should I be on my way?"

I gripped his arm. "I know you're only joking, but I'm worried enough about my mom that I'm not going to risk it. I hadn't started a fire today, and it's getting cold in the living room. I need to heat it up before the chill gets to her and freezes up her lungs."

Eli nodded in understanding, his expression immediately turning serious.

He dropped his jacket on a nearby chair and stared at Mom's lifeless body.

"No need to be careful about making noise," I told him as he cautiously made his way to the fireplace. "She's a heavy sleeper. I'd rather she stay asleep until we have the place heated, anyway."

"Got it. Are there any other fireplaces in the house?"

"There's one in my bedroom."

"Go throw some wood on it and get one started up there. Always better to have one upstairs and one down when it's this cold. Make sure to use the screen to prevent a bigger fire."

"Won't we run out of firewood quicker that way?"

He glanced at the couch. "There's definitely not enough space for two people to sleep on that, so unless you want to freeze in your sleep—"

"I'll be fine."

"It wasn't a request, Emily," he replied firmly.

I took the pile of firewood he handed me, momentarily stunned into silence. I wasn't used to someone bossing me around, least of all a guy I barely knew. I was disconcerted to discover that I kind of liked it. Liking it went against everything I believed. However, Eli was trying to help so that got him brownie points.

That was sweet, in its own way, though the method through which he was demonstrating he cared could do with some improvement.

Fifteen minutes later, I was tending to the fledgling fire in my bedroom when I heard footsteps creaking along the hallway outside my door.

"I'm in here," I called out, guessing the footsteps belonged to Eli. He crept in and joined me, kneeling, by the fire.

"Not bad," he commented. "I underestimated you."

"Which turned out great for me, considering my mom and I would be screwed if you hadn't."

He chuckled. "I guess so."

"How's the fire doing downstairs?"

"Crackling away. It'll get hot soon."

"Same with this one. How often should I come up to check it to make sure it hasn't burned out if I'm downstairs?"

Eli appeared to consider my question. "Probably every hour or so. Most of the time you won't have to give it any new wood. It will just need poking and prodding a bit."

"Good to know."

An awkward silence filled the air before it became apparent that neither of us knew what to say. Eli's stomach rumbled, and the tension immediately broke.

I burst out laughing. "Are you hungry?"

He ran a hand through his hair. "Maybe."

"Guess it's your good fortune because I was going to make spaghetti for dinner. We're in luck because the stove is run by gas. Care to help? If not, you can sit in the kitchen and watch if you want."

"I'm sure I can work up the energy to cook with you." The look in his eyes was hungry but not necessarily for food.

His gaze drifted over me, my body heating with each visual caress.

We made our way to the kitchen just as my mom woke up in the living room. She looked at us with sleepy, confused eyes.

"Emily, who's that with you? Is that Paxton Cooper?"

"Eli," he laughed.

"All you boys look the same."

"Other than Paxton, you're not wrong. How are you feeling, Judy?"

She yawned. "Stiff. Hungry. Did the power go off?"

"An hour ago," I replied. "And a good thing you're hungry because we're about to make dinner."

My mom looked at me curiously, "Are you going to tell me why Eli Cooper is visiting?"

"Oh," I said. "He was worried we didn't have any way to keep the house warm, which is just as well because we ran out of firewood."

She beamed at him. "Thank you, Eli. You didn't have to do that."

"I couldn't leave you out on a limb, and I knew it had been a while since Paxton had been around with firewood, so …"

"Speaking of, is there any reason you came around this time? It is normally Paxton who looks in on the seniors."

"He came to see me," I said without thinking, glancing at Eli out of the corner of my eye. His nod confirmed my statement.

My mother looked more ecstatic than I had seen her look in a long time. "I hope you've invited him to stay for dinner, Emily."

"Naturally. He's going to help me make it."

"Even better."

"I'll make you some tea while we're in the kitchen," I called over my shoulder as I gently tugged Eli's sleeve, pulling him into the kitchen.

"Thank you, honey. Cream and—"

"Two sugars. I know, Ma."

When we entered the kitchen, Eli seemed surprised to discover I'd already made the bulk of the sauce.

With a dip of a nearby spoon, he tasted it. "It's bland."

I rolled my eyes. "The way my mom likes it. If I had it my way, it would be spicy and garlicky as hell."

He set the spoon in the sink. "Sounds wonderful. How about I divide it up? A portion for your mom, and I can spice up the rest for us?"

"That would be great. Can you do that while I cut up the vegetables and put the spaghetti on to boil?"

Eli moved over to take charge of the sauce as I maneuvered around him to complete everything else. It was such a common thing—people cooking together—but I found myself thoroughly enjoying the activity.

"Here, try this," Eli said after a while, dipping a spoon into the sauce and holding it out for me to taste. I blew on it before licking it, and all but moaned in delight.

"That's delicious. Do you cook much for yourself?"

He didn't seem to be listening. His eyes were on my mouth, staring intently at my lips. It made me blush furiously.

"Eli."

"Yes?"

On impulse, I leaned in and kissed him, relishing the look of surprise on his face.

"Do you cook much?" I asked again when I pulled away.

"Um … yes. I do. When I can, anyway," His breath hitched, coming faster than before. He reached forward and pushed the hair that had fallen in my eyes away. "Why did you do that?"

I licked the taste of him from my lips. "Are you telling me I can't?"

"Absolutely not. Are you telling me I can?" He leaned in and brushed his lips against mine, so briefly, I wasn't sure if it actually happened.

"It's not like you asked for permission the first time."

"You didn't complain."

The memory of their first kiss sent shivers racing down her spine to settle in her core. "Don't embarrass me in front of my mom, and I'll consider more kisses."

He grinned foolishly. "Deal."

That evening, I had the best meal I'd had since arriving in Frazier Falls, and Eli was a perfect gentleman. He declined my mom's offer to stay over, claiming he needed to go in order to get back home before it got too late.

When I showed him to the door, I more than expected him to kiss me.

He leaned in as I was getting ready to pucker my lips and whispered, "I'll call you tomorrow."

"Are you trying to play the long game with a woman who's only around because of a bit of snow?"

He laughed. "Maybe. I'm probably being stupid."

"Probably." My insides warmed at the thought of Eli wanting more.

He grazed the pad of his thumb over my lower lip. "I'll talk to you tomorrow, Emily."

A strong, heavy heartbeat thumped inside my chest.

"I look forward to it." I was shocked to discover that I meant it.

CHAPTER ELEVEN

ELI

I woke up to sunlight streaming through my bedroom window. Given that I didn't have work today, I chose to sleep in, which made waking up midmorning even better. But the sunshine meant more than simply the promise of a good day.

It meant Emily would likely be heading back to California soon.

I was past the point of pretending I didn't like her. There were no two ways about it. I was crazy attracted to her, barbed tongue and all. That was the most fun part of her besides her kisses. She gave as good as she got.

If today was going to be the last day I could spend time with her, then I'd be crazy not to get up and seize the moment.

I dialed her phone before I had the chance to rethink what I was doing.

After the phone rang five times, I wondered if she might still be asleep. Maybe I wasn't the only one sleeping in.

But then she picked up.

"Hello? Eli?" Her tone was chipper and friendly.

"Morning, Emily," I let out too quickly. "I'm sorry if I woke you."

"No, I was working. It's fine."

"Working? I thought you couldn't while you were stuck here?"

"Nah, I got some stuff sent over that I could work on remotely," she replied. "Anyway, did you need something?"

There was a lift on the last word, was that hope I heard in her voice?

"Um …" I trailed off. If she was working, then I didn't want to disturb her. "I wanted to ask if you wanted to head out for coffee somewhere, but if you're busy, I don't want—"

"Oh, that sounds great," she cut in, her voice as bright as the sun piercing my blinds. "I could use a coffee. Ma's all out. Though, I can't stay out for long because of this project I'm working on. I do love a paycheck, and no work means no check."

"We could make it a working coffee break if you want," I suggested, thinking that this way I could spend more time with her. "Sit in companionable silence while we do our own thing…"

"Seriously? You'd be okay with that?"

"God knows I could get out of my house, and I'm sure you feel the same way about your mom's. Besides, the coffee at Alice's is actually great."

"It's a date then," she replied.

I could practically see her smiling down the phone.

"Is it?" My insides swirled with excitement.

"You know what I mean. Do you feel like picking me up?"

"Sure, I always pick up my dates."

Twenty minutes later, I waited outside Judy Flanagan's house. After a single knock on the door, Emily joined me. We were back in my truck in seconds flat.

"Brrr, is it colder out despite the sun? I'm absolutely Baltic."

I raised an eyebrow, "Baltic? Like the sea?"

Emily laughed as I pulled the truck away, heading toward Alice's. "It's slang for freezing."

"I've never heard someone say that before."

She shrugged, a graceful movement of one shoulder. "I think it's more of an Irish and Scottish thing. My ma says it all the time. Guess she's rubbing off on me."

"I'll be sure to use it to describe how cold I am to my brothers. I can't wait to see their confused faces."

"No, that'll make you look weird and desperate."

"How did you reach that conclusion?" I gave her a cursory glance, cocking my head in question.

"Because it looks like you're making an effort to speak like me. You only get to be Irish by birth, not by choice." Her laugh rang through the air like sweet music.

"One day a year, everyone gets to be Irish. That day, I drink green beer, see leprechauns, and wish on four-leaf clovers."

She laughed. "I hope you only see the leprechauns after the beer."

"It takes about four or five before they appear." I pulled down Main Street and parked in the only free spot in front of the diner. "We're here."

"That didn't take long."

"It's a small town. What did you expect?"

"Right. A small town …"

We made our way into Alice's, which was reasonably busy—likely full of people desperate to get out of their houses like Emily and me. A couple left one of the window tables as I set eyes on it. Emily took the initiative and rushed over to claim it as ours. Somehow, this only served to endear her all the more in my eyes. She was eager for our time together.

I took the seat across from her as Alice approached. "Hey, kids. What will it be?"

"Two coffees, please, Alice." I looked across the table. "This is Emily Flanagan."

"You're Judy's daughter."

"Yes, ma'am." Emily pushed the dirty dishes from the last couple to the edge of the table.

Cassy Reilly swung by and swept them up.

"How is your mom?"

Emily's smile faltered as the tension tightened the delicate features of her face. "She's hanging in there. The cold isn't helping her much, but I'd say she's on the mend."

"Glad to hear it. I'll send some pie home with you. Judy loves my cherry pie."

"That sounds great. She'll appreciate that."

I raised a hand before Alice could disappear. "I don't think Emily's had your pie. Can we have a slice of apple and cherry so she can try them both?"

"I'll get that going for you." Alice turned on her high-top tennis shoes, the soles squeaking against the worn wood.

"What about those floors, Alice?" I looked down at the wood that had a path worn into it.

"Not fixin' what's not broken," she called back.

When I turned back to Emily, she'd already pulled her computer and a notebook from her bag.

"What is it you actually do?" I asked, suddenly curious.

She raised her head and looked over the screen. "I'm an urban planner in Los Angeles."

My eyes opened wide. I hadn't considered she'd be somehow connected with building and growth. Once again, we had another thing in common. "How in the world did you get into that line of work?"

"I studied geography and sociology at Berkeley."

"Fancy."

"I tried my hand at becoming a meteorologist." She winced as if the thought was painful. "But that didn't work out."

I sat up straight, more intrigued than ever. "Meteorologist? As in—"

"A weather girl, yes. Laugh all you want."

"Do you see me laughing?" I kept my face deadpan and neutral, but then I ruined it by letting out a burst of laughter despite myself.

Emily giggled in response, which was possibly the most adorable sound I'd ever heard.

"I know, it doesn't seem like the right kind of job for me, given my temperament. However, I love my current job, so I guess it's all good."

I glanced down at Emily's notebook and all the scribbles that didn't make sense. I couldn't make heads nor tails of it.

"What are you working on now?"

Alice dropped off our order.

"Thanks," I said as Emily's eyes lit up when she saw the pie.

She grabbed a forkful right away.

"Excellent choice of baked goods," she murmured in delight around a massive bite of apple pie.

"You have … you've got filling on your face," I said, reaching over to swipe it off with my thumb. Her tongue darted out at the same time. Feeling it against my skin sent a shiver of desire racing through me.

She blushed slightly when I brought the dab of filling to my mouth and licked it clean. "Maybe you should wait, and you can lick my face when I'm done," she teased.

"I'm game." Seeing as my pants were growing uncomfortably tight, I turned the conversation away from her tongue and licking to her work. "What is it you're working on?"

"A park, actually," she said, turning her tablet around so I could see the screen. "I'm not the one architecturally designing the park, but I'm working out the logistics of where it goes and what we want in it."

"Owen's designed a couple parks before."

Emily perked up at that. "Your older brother?"

I nodded. "He's an architect by trade."

"Wow, and you all run a construction company together?"

"Yes, but Owen designs all the new builds that we do when the client hasn't attached an architect to their project already. He has his Green House Project, which he's been rolling out across the United States for the past half a year. It's beginning to gain traction in Europe now, too."

"Wait a second," Emily interrupted, holding a hand up to emphasize her request. "Are you telling me that your brother Owen is the one behind the Green House Project? The one responsible for all those eco-friendly, sustainable apartments currently being built in Sacramento?"

"That would be the one. You've heard about it?"

"Have I heard about it?" Emily parroted back incredulously. "Our department has been trying to get the funds together to offer a joint project to Owen for a couple of months now. I never thought we'd get the money, so it's been on the back burner."

There was a certain kind of irony that somehow, someway, Emily and I were destined to meet. "It's a small world. Almost seems like fate that you've been stuck here. A shame Owen and Rich are still trapped in New York. But you know what?" I forked a bite of cherry pie and chewed, giving her time to respond.

Emily perked up. "What?" she said with renewed excitement.

"You could talk to Carla about it. She's Owen's fiancée, and the reason the project got any investors in the first place. Given the snow, she's likely to have some time."

Emily glanced out of the window. "If it stays settled like this for another day or so, then I'll have to head back."

"Then I guess we'll have to hope for more snow."

Her expression was mutinous. "Don't even joke about it. I'm on thin ice as it is with this extended leave of absence. My job is on the line if I don't get back soon."

I felt a twinge of disappointment at the thought. Though I knew that Emily wasn't going to stay in Frazier Falls, something inside me had hoped for the possibility.

She lifted her cup and breathed in the aroma before she took a sip and sighed. "If I have to head back before getting the opportunity to meet Carla, I don't suppose you could help me set up a phone or video conference with her, could you? You know, to brainstorm ideas."

"That's not a problem." I was happy to help Emily in any way I could. It seemed like I'd been trying to help her out since that first day when I told her to ask Pax to get the potatoes. While we hadn't gotten off to a good start, things were turning out better than I'd expected.

The two of us worked in companionable silence for an hour or so. After that, we were content to slowly chip away at our coffees and our work. Though I didn't strictly have any work to do, it felt satisfying to make some decent headway with all the tax forms due to be completed for the year.

It occurred to me that if Emily ended up working with the Green House Project, she'd inevitably come back to Frazier Falls more frequently than the few visits a year she'd normally take to see her mother. It meant the two of us could possibly explore more.

No doubt, I was getting ahead of myself. I barely knew the woman. How could I realistically think about having more? A future where she lived in Los Angeles, and I lived in Frazier Falls was not a great option, but it was better than nothing.

I looked up from my paperwork to watch her. The sun shone through the window onto her red hair. It looked like dancing flames with touches of red and orange and gold.

She hummed under her breath as she worked happily writing away in her own world—a world I wanted to be a part of.

Emily working by my side, doing her own thing while I did mine, felt right. If I had been sitting here in Alice's working by myself, I would have felt completely alone.

Her presence changed my entire perspective. Had I been content to live by myself? To have no significant other to share things with? Nobody to walk through the forest with? Nobody to cook with? No one to kiss or fall asleep with? My life until now suddenly seemed unremarkable and sad. Worse yet, was that my time with Emily had an expiration date.

I chuckled at the irony of it all, which garnered a curiously raised brow from her.

Trust me to find something that I wanted just as it was about to go away. For now, I had to take each minute, and hour, and day, as it came. I refused to let the time I had with her get spoiled with pointless negative thinking.

"Would you like another coffee?" I asked about an hour into our work session. "Or lunch?" I asked when the clock in Alice's hit two in the afternoon.

A sudden luminous smile lit up her face. "Absolutely."

CHAPTER TWELVE

EMILY

When my phone vibrated noisily against the grain of my mom's old wooden desk, I almost ignored it ... almost. Then I saw it was from my boss. I accepted the call, feeling guilty about my intent to disregard it in the first place.

"Don, hi!" I said too quickly. "Sorry, I nearly missed this. I was too engrossed in the park project to notice my phone." Could he hear the lie in my voice?

"That's always a good sign, though not as good a sign as you actually being back in the office, Emily."

I analyzed his tone for irritation. "You know I'd be back there in a flash if it were possible."

"I don't doubt how desperate you are to get back, though I know how worried you are about your mom's health. It can't be an easy situation. Add in the weather, and I'm sure it's pure misery."

The universe had blessed me with a compassionate, understanding boss. Don Cleaver was the kind of supervisor a person could only dream of having—polite, driven, organized, and a good listener.

Upon discovering my mom was unwell and knowing that Colorado was facing its coldest winter in thirty years, he had all but marched me to the airport and put me on a flight to Frazier Falls. Don was a saint. His boss, Pete Rosen, was not.

Ma always said that shite rolled downhill, but somehow Don always managed to make it stop at him, which created an ideal work environment for me. However, my three weeks paid vacation had expired nine days ago, and I wasn't sure how ideal this situation could remain.

"Don, the weather is awful, and I hate it here," I complained, which was mostly true. I didn't want to think about Eli, because then I'd have to admit that there was something, or rather someone besides my mother, worth hanging around for. "It gets better for a day or so, taunting me with the possibility of leaving; then the storms move in again. A couple of folks from here managed to fly to Europe a week ago, but they've been stuck in New York trying to return to Colorado ever since." A woeful sigh escaped. "Though being stuck in New York sounds much better than being stuck in Colorado. I don't even know how they managed to make it to the airport, in all honesty. The roads are piled high with snow. White walls line the highway for miles."

Don laughed. "Some people are simply luckier than others, or unlucky, as the case may be. But there's no point in constantly waiting day by day on the off chance you might be able to leave. I don't want you to risk life or limb to catch a flight."

My heart beat wildly in my chest. "What are you saying?" My heart pumped hard.

"I'm saying that I'm giving you two more weeks to get back. Unpaid, though. I can't justify the time as it is, but I know you need it."

"Is Peter threatening to fire me?" The thought of not having a job terrified me. If I thought things were bad now, a lack of income would only be a straight dive into hell.

"If you can get back before that time, that would be great, but I've got your back until then."

While the offer was great, something about it didn't feel right. "Do you want me to keep working on the park project?"

"No, I can't ask you to work when you're on unpaid leave, so I'd suggest not working. However, if the choice is between doing work and being bored to death, then be my guest and toil away."

Don was his chipper self, but I had to know if he was masking something more serious. "Does Pete know you're doing this?"

The silence said it all. "He's putting on the pressure to let you go. I offered up the two weeks you have left and told him it was part of The Family and Medical Leave Act to appease him."

My heart shook and rattled. "What happens if I still can't get back in two weeks?"

He sighed. "We'll cross that bridge when we come to it. In all honesty, we can barely afford to have you away as long as you've been, but it's not as if we can control the weather. I'll do my best to keep your job safe."

"Thank you," I replied, genuinely grateful. I checked the time. "Okay, I better get going, or else my mom will complain that lunch is late."

"I'm sure she won't complain too much. She's got you there to look after her."

"That's where you're wrong," I joked. "She's getting spoiled and is too used to having me around to bark orders at. She's living the life of luxury, I tell you."

"Get back to your daughterly duties. Fingers crossed, we get you back before the twentieth."

I shook my head. "I can't believe we're into February already. Where has the time gone?"

"To Frazier Falls, clearly."

We said our goodbyes, and I hung up the phone feeling conflicted.

I was happy to have a boss who was concerned for my well-being. He wasn't shouting or screaming for me to get back to California this instant, but the underlying threat was there. His boss was aware of my absence, and that didn't bode well for me long-term.

I dialed Sadie.

"Hey," she whispered. "Everything okay?"

"Why are you whispering?"

I could hear the squeaky wheels of her chair, and pictured her sliding close to her desk, hunkering down inside her cubicle. "Pete is here, and he's not happy. Apparently, none of us work hard enough, and heads are going to roll."

I touch the back of my neck, feeling the guillotine already. "Oh, hell." I was on my way to living in a box on the corner of Wiltshire and Vine. "I'll be the first to go. Easier to can someone if they're not there to cry and plead."

"No way, he's been giving Don the stink eye. Apparently, he's moving too slowly on the park project."

My gut ached. "What about you, are you going to be okay? I mean … don't take this the wrong way, but you spend most of your day watching Netflix and texting your latest boy toy." Sadie was the woman's equivalent to a man whore, which made her a whore, but that didn't sound flattering.

"I'm fine. I may be lazy, but I'm a total kiss ass, and he likes the weekly lattes I show up with." She giggled. "I'm telling you, a double shot with hot milk and a Splenda goes a long way."

"You're so bad."

The squeak of the wheels sounded again. "Shit, he's on his way back, I've got to go."

Before she hung up, I heard her sugary-sweet voice say, "Mr. Rosen, can I get you a latte?"

With Don negotiating two additional weeks, I should have been fine, but I didn't feel fine. I felt trapped. If I had to be trapped in Frazier Falls, there was at least a silver lining. I got to see my mom for longer, and it gave me more time to spend with Eli.

I burst out laughing though nobody was here to hear the sound. "A silver lining?" Last week I was in hell. Eli wasn't a silver lining, that man was trouble dressed in fitted jeans and a parka. "The sooner I leave, the better."

Don't think about Eli.

Don't think about Eli.

It was fine chanting inside my head to stop thinking about him. It was another thing entirely to stop obsessing over him.

He was smart.

He was handsome.

He was bitingly funny.

He was as jaded as me.

And yet he cared about people, and looked out for them, and drove through snowstorms to ensure my mother wouldn't freeze to death.

He was a good cook and happy to sit in silence and work away at his own thing. When he thought I wasn't looking, and sometimes when I clearly was, he stared at me like I was the most beautiful person he'd ever seen.

Merely thinking about the way he looked at me caused my face to heat up.

Being around him made me feel young. The way I did when I was a teen, longing to grab the guy I liked and drag him behind the bleachers to make out. Damn, I was even picking up his stupid similes. So much for me ribbing him for wanting to use Irish slang. I was becoming Eli Cooper with red hair and boobs.

"Emily, I think whatever you were cooking in the kitchen is probably ready," my mom called from downstairs.

I knew when the casserole I had cooking in the oven would be ready because I'd set a timer on my phone for it. There was still ten minutes left.

"Talk about impatient," I mumbled under my breath.

Resolving to record my mom being pushy about mealtimes at least once over the next two weeks as evidence for Don, I wandered down the stairs, past my mom in the living room, and through to the kitchen. To my surprise, she followed me, dragging her oxygen tank behind, the wheeze and hiss was an ever-present reminder that she wasn't a hundred percent.

"You seem to be in a good mood, sweetheart," she said as I opened the oven door to check on the casserole.

"Yep, this definitely needs another ten minutes," I said, mostly to myself, before glancing at my mom. "What did you say?"

"That your spirits seem high. Did something happen?"

"Um, my boss called."

"A normal person wouldn't associate that with being a good thing. Is he being supportive about being stuck here so long?"

"He was understanding." I tamped down the need to vent. Unloading my stress on my mom wasn't good for her. Hell, it wasn't good for me. "But, his boss is pressing for my return." She shrugged as if it wasn't a big deal. "No worries, Don's got my back." *God, I hope he does.*

"I'm glad you have a good boss," my mom said as she sat at the breakfast bar, content to watch me collect bowls and silverware and glasses for lunch. "Did he say anything about when you have to go back?"

"He's actually given me another two weeks."

My mom brightened up immediately. "That's great."

"It's unpaid, though, and he can't guarantee my job after that," I explained, "so I can't stay for two weeks if I can get back before then."

"That's ... okay. I understand." The excitement that had bounced off her moments ago suddenly went flat. "You can't afford to lose your job." She hung her head. "I'm embarrassed to say that I can't afford for you to lose your job, either."

Ma got her citizenship years ago and paid into the social security system, but it didn't give much back. There was no way she could live off less than a grand a month. Thankfully the house was paid off, or she'd be in a pickle, then again maybe it wasn't such a good thing. If mom couldn't afford to live in Frazier Falls, she'd be forced to move back to Los Angeles.

It did no good to dwell on what-ifs.

"You're right, I can't afford to forfeit a paycheck for weeks on end, and I can't lose my job. I have rent to pay and my student loans and—"

Ma raised her hand. "It's okay, honey, you don't have to explain yourself." A smile graced her lips, but it didn't reach her eyes. She never wanted to be a burden. "I always knew your life was going to be far bigger than mine. Why do you think I moved us to a city? A small town wouldn't provide you with enough opportunity."

I paused before speaking. She'd never told me why she left the city. I'd assumed she and Mary wanted a change of pace—snail's pace wasn't possible in San Francisco or Los Angeles unless you were stuck in traffic. "Thank you for your sacrifice."

She most likely felt about the city, the way I felt about Frazier Falls.

She breathed deeply several times. "You're the most important person in the world to me. Who else would I make a decision like that for? Sometimes, you have to make the big decisions for love."

"I moved to the city because you weren't going to get the opportunities I knew you deserved back in Ardmore. You needed a fresh start way more than I did. Once I knew you'd be all right, I thought of me. Frazier Falls is exactly where I want to stay."

My eyes stung with the threat of tears. I didn't look at her. Instead, I focused on setting the table for lunch. "I understand."

She made a sound of discontent. "Do you?"

"What do you mean?" My insides twisted with tension.

"Sometimes you have to look further ahead, beyond the next paycheck. What about other opportunities? What about love?"

A quick glance told me she was dreaming of white dresses and buttercream frosted cakes.

"I have love. I love you … and shoes."

"Shoes, don't rub your feet at night."

I turned my back and rolled my eyes. Ma was still spry enough to chuck me upside the head for being disrespectful.

"You haven't broken in a pair of Jimmy Choos. Those will rub your feet raw night or day."

She let out a growl that turned into a coughing fit.

I got her a glass of water, and as soon as she took a drink, she blurted out the name, "Eli."

My heart raced. "What about him?"

"I'd say that's a pretty great opportunity."

"I'm not following you," I lied.

"Yes, you are. You're just being stubborn."

"Wonder who I got that from?"

"Emily."

I gave my mom a level stare. "He's a guy, Ma. Another guy who lives in a town that doesn't offer what I need. What you need."

Her hazel eyes dimmed as if I'd flipped the switch to her internal light off. "I feel sorry for you if you genuinely think that, honey. Not every man struggles through a snowstorm to make sure you're doing okay."

"One good deed doesn't make him the right man for me. It just means he was nice that one time."

She rolled her eyes. "Honestly, Emily, I don't think I've ever seen you look at a man the way you looked at Eli the other night when he came around. When he was outside picking you up for coffee, you absolutely glowed. You like him. You'd do well to admit that to yourself."

I stared at the floor. "Don't make things harder for me than they already are."

"If it's making your decision to leave Frazier Falls harder, then that's only because you have feelings for him and know that I'm speaking the truth. Otherwise, there would be nothing to debate. You'd be able to head back to Los Angeles with a clear head."

"Ma—"

She held up a hand. "There's no point in discussing this any further. The casserole must be ready by now." She stared past me to the oven.

Mom's tone said it all. She'd made her point, and my defense had been weak and futile.

What was all this angst over a sarcastic construction worker who lived in a tiny town?

While that barely scratched the surface of who or what Eli Cooper was, at his core, it was true. I was a city girl who went out for cocktails on a Wednesday evening and likely knew more people by name than there were people in Frazier Falls.

And regardless of what made Eli who he was, he was the reason I was faltering. The reason I was happy and excited to be stuck here longer. The reason going back to Los Angeles might be painful, although necessary.

So much for the headstrong woman I was. Right now, I felt like a chew toy for two dogs. On one side was a loyal lab who loved me unconditionally, and wanted the best for me, it didn't hurt that in my head he had Eli's eyes and his strength of presence. On the other side, tugging in equal measure was my job, which snarled and snapped, making sure it got its fair share of flesh.

Yes, I was torn, but given the situation, there was only one option. Fall for Eli today, and leave him when I had too. Who said a girl couldn't have everything? I might not be able to keep it, but wasn't a taste better than none at all?

CHAPTER THIRTEEN

ELI

I was out of milk again. By that, I meant out of everything. I had to stop waiting until my kitchen was barren before buying food.

Considering the weather, I suppose I could forgive myself. Nobody in their right mind would go outside in a blizzard for milk but leave it to me to wait until things were dire.

Owen and Rich were still in New York. I was beginning to worry about my older brother. It was fine feeling claustrophobic from being inside all day in Frazier Falls; it was another thing entirely for Owen to feel trapped in New York where his panic attacks began.

Heaving a heavy sigh, I laced up my boots and threw on my jacket, grateful that the Cooper Construction truck was in my driveway. With Owen gone, and the weather still miserable, it was all but impossible to fulfill the orders we were supposed to start in February.

Thankfully, our clients were all affected by the weather, and understanding when it came to the delay.

I was getting restless and impatient, and I wanted to get back to work simply to keep busy. With a low laugh, I thought of Emily, who'd been desperately trying to get back to work for weeks.

A sudden flash of empathy overtook me for a moment. Here I was going crazy, and my job was practically on my doorstep, while hers was a thousand miles away.

I shivered as I ran out to the truck, brushing snow off my shoulders when I opened the door and sat down. Even though the journey would only take me a couple of minutes, I cranked up the heat, intending to keep the engine running when I went into Wilkes Corner Store. I thought longingly of the large super-market in Idaho Springs, or the one in Indian Springs. If I'd been able to drive there to buy my groceries, then I wouldn't keep running out of everything week after week. Sadly, it would take too long to get out there, with no guarantee the roads were safe enough to do so.

When I entered, I was surprised to see Rachel behind the register, hovering close to a space heater as she read a magazine.

She smiled when she saw me.

"Hello there, Eli. Another horrible evening, it seems."

"Definitely. I thought my brother might have been helping you out, given the weather." I returned her smile.

"I'm right over here," Pax called out from the far aisle, startling me. "I'm helping Lucy with her grocery shopping; then I'm going to take Rachel home."

"You came by to shop just in time," Rachel said. "I'm about to close up for the night."

"Perfect timing." I moved down the aisle, pushing a small cart in front of me. "Evening, Lucy," I murmured when I spied her behind Pax.

Lucy was in her fifties, with a full face of makeup and perox-ide-blond hair that was always kept tied back in an immaculate up-do, even when she wasn't going anywhere. Her winter jacket seemed more fashionable than practical with its white fur collar.

Her husband had passed away a few years ago, and ever since then, Pax had helped her with all the chores Burt used to do.

Though she definitely abused his help. She had him replace her generator when the old one was perfectly fine. We assumed it was to ogle Pax, but he didn't seem to mind. After all, he helped everyone.

Lucy always cooked for him, which was something Pax professed to be terrible at. I was fairly certain it was because he never had a good enough reason to learn, given how many of the older ladies in Frazier Falls fed him.

I had to admit it was a pretty good deal. He never had to buy food. On the other hand, he was in the grocery store more often than anybody else, which seemed somewhat ironic.

"Good evening, Eli," Lucy crooned as she threw some bags of rice and pasta into the shopping cart Pax was pushing along. "You don't look like you're in such a great mood."

I tried to smile, but it fell flat. "It's this weather. It's gone on for too long. I live two minutes from here, and I still had to drive."

Lucy laughed. "I'd have thought you'd be feeling better, what with all the time you've been spending with Judy's girl."

Pax hid a smirk behind his hand at the comment.

I threw a disgruntled look his way.

"Seems like someone's been gossiping about his brother's business," I bit out.

"Oh, don't be so defensive," Lucy said with a wave of her hand. "It's good for you boys to be settling down. First Owen, now you. Although, what will I do when my dear Paxton finds a woman? I'll have nobody to mow my lawn or help around the house."

"I can't see anyone being able to put up with him, so I'm sure you don't have to worry."

"Charming," Pax pretended to lob a bag of beans my way but dropped them into the cart instead.

Lucy sighed. "And here I was hoping Paxton would fall for my Rose." She patted his arm. "To have you as a son-in-law … now that would be ideal."

Pax turned away so Lucy couldn't see the horrified expression on his face. It confused me for a moment, but then I vaguely recalled how Rose Rogers had picked on Pax when they were in middle school, back when he was mostly silent.

No wonder he didn't like the idea of marrying her.

"I'm happy being single, Lucy," Pax said quietly, reaching over for some canned corn as he spoke.

"Oh, nonsense. Nobody is happy being single. What I wouldn't give to have my Burt back." She pinned me with a look. "Eli, help me out. You feel much better now that you're with Emily, right?"

I was with Emily, but I wasn't *with* Emily. There was no doubt that she'd trade me for a plane ticket as soon as the weather cleared. That realization felt like a fist to my chest.

"I think you're getting ahead of yourself," I interrupted, laughing awkwardly. "Emily and I aren't going out. She'll be heading back to Los Angeles any day now. We're spending some time together so that we don't die of boredom."

Lucy raised a knowing eyebrow. "That's how it always starts. Everyone makes excuses when they like someone, then, before you know it, you're in love, and there's nothing you can do about it."

Pax let out a deep belly laugh. "Trust you to fall for a woman who'll end up running away from you."

My scowl made the space between my eyebrows ache. "We're just friends."

"It didn't seem that way when you ran out to help her during the power outage."

Lucy's eyes widened, as did Rachel's over by the register.

Clearly, she was eavesdropping on the whole conversation. I couldn't blame her. It wasn't as if there was anything else interesting happening in town. Was there a bet at the knitting club or the on-hiatus walking club about us? Anyone who bet on the longevity of our "relationship" would go away a loser.

"I was worried about Judy," I explained, which was half of the truth. "Her house isn't equipped for a winter this bad."

"I've been telling her for years now that she needs to get a backup generator, and those windows need updating, too." Lucy pulled her cart down the aisle, dragging Pax along with her. "She needs to look after herself. Her health isn't getting any better, and she's not getting any younger. Thank you for looking out for her, Eli."

I smiled. "Not a problem."

"He stayed for dinner when he went over," Pax said, reveling in stirring the gossip pot further. "I'm surprised he didn't spend the night, considering the weather."

I growled in exasperation. Pax had found his voice today, and that made him impossible to deal with. I glanced at the time. "As wonderful as this conversation is, I need to get on with my shopping before Rachel closes up the store. I'll see you in the office tomorrow, Pax."

A frown slipped across his face. "Why do we need to go in?"

"We need to work out an alternative plan of action for the rest of February, given the weather. Owen and Rich still aren't back, so I could do with everyone who works with me and is in Frazier Falls to be present. Which means you."

He nodded in understanding. "Got it. See you in the morning, then."

I smiled at Lucy. "Have a lovely evening."

"I will. Rose is going to video-call me, so here's hoping the storm doesn't affect the connection."

I left the pair of them in order to venture over to the picked-through produce aisle. This weather needed to get better. Long-ingly, I thought of ripe tomatoes, potatoes with smooth, unblem-ished skin, fresh lettuce, and spring onions.

"So much for asking Emily around to make dinner," I muttered under my breath. I'd been hoping to invite her over the following evening, but I felt as if anything I tried to cook would be disap-pointing. With the weight of resignation weighing me down, I slogged through the rest of my shopping in a worse mood than I'd started.

When I got back to my truck, I was welcomed by a hug of heat. By the time I reached my driveway, I didn't want to leave the cab. I was content to sit there with the engine off until the heat in the car dissipated. Eventually, the interior grew cold enough that I found the willpower to grab my meager supplies, get out of the truck, and make my way through the gusting wind and snow to my front door.

My boots were tossed aside in the entryway before I tucked my groceries away and headed straight for the couch, not caring about the snow on my clothes, which rapidly melted into the leather. Sleepiness overtook me.

Had I known I was going to feel like this, I'd have put off shop-ping until tomorrow in favor of an early night.

I pulled my phone out of my pocket, yawning, and checked if any of the restaurants in Frazier Falls were planning to open this week, but all of them stated that they were closed until the weather cleared.

"I can't even take Emily out," I grumbled.

Here I was, trying to organize one semi-decent date for the two of us before she left, and Frazier Falls seemed to be conspiring against me.

This wouldn't happen if I'd stayed in a city. For the first time, I felt dissatisfied with where I lived. Feeling that way was stupid and pointless. Colorado was considered high desert, and this type of prolonged weather was an anomaly. For ninety-nine percent of my life, I'd never had a complaint about Frazier Falls. If I hadn't met Emily, I wouldn't be pissed off now. But I had met her, and that changed everything.

I glanced at my phone. Emily and I had been texting back and forth for the past few days about nothing in particular. The communication was comforting and fun despite the lack of real content. Maybe it was because it wasn't about anything important. We were merely talking to each other for the sake of talking—the way a person did when they were getting to know someone.

Lucy's and Paxton's jibes still rung in my ears. I did like Emily —a lot—but what could I do about it? I'd only be making things more difficult if I announced that I liked her too much for her to go back to California.

Even if she liked me as much as I did her, Emily loved her job more. She loved California. I didn't blame her. At the end of the day, I'd never leave Frazier Falls or my job for anyone. I couldn't expect her to choose me.

It was unfair and wildly unfortunate for the two of us to have met when we did. If the weather hadn't been as bad as it was, none of this would have even happened in the first place.

Regret filled my thoughts. Could I honestly say that never meeting Emily would be better than having met her and half fallen for her?

Shaking my head in frustration, I rolled from my sofa, took off my jacket, and headed for the kitchen.

"Time for another frozen pizza," I mumbled. What I needed was to get over Emily Flanagan; for her benefit and mine.

CHAPTER FOURTEEN

EMILY

Shopping at Wilkes' had reached its limit long ago in terms of variety. A trip to the nearest supermarket had been exactly what I needed to get out of my mom's house and Frazier Falls for an afternoon.

I'd never enjoyed walking the aisles so much.

The weather hadn't gotten better, per se, but there had been a break in the storm long enough for me to drive the hour or so out to the store in Indian Springs, spend another hour shopping, then make it back to town. When I was fifteen miles away, snowflakes as big as cotton balls fell from the sky, and the wind picked up again.

"Oh, great," I said sarcastically. "Just what I need. Couldn't wait fifteen bloody miles, could you?" I glared up through the sunroof of my mom's car with an accusatory stare meant for the storm.

I hoped against hope I would make it back okay. I had food in the car that needed to be put away. At least with the cold, stuff would be fine given that the temperature outside was like a freezer, but that was beside the point. The shopping wouldn't get back to my mom's if I didn't.

I thought of everything I'd bought and wondered if Eli would be up for helping me cook again. That way, I could make something plain for my mom, and we could eat something spicy. Mexican food, maybe. Or Italian, or Indian.

My mouth watered at the mere thought, but in order to cook anything, I had to get home, which was steadily becoming more difficult as the snow covered the road thick and fast.

Twenty minutes later, I'd made it to the edge of town. As I began to breathe a sigh of relief, the car made an unsettling, spluttering noise.

"Oh, no, that can't be good." I willed it to last a few more minutes. The noise grew more guttural, the engine struggled, and the car moved slower and slower with every curse that escaped my lips. "Without bad luck, I'd have no luck at all."

All I could do was steer to the edge of a sidewalk as it coughed and sputtered to a stop. I looked through the flurry of snow and saw nothing recognizable. The houses were unfamiliar, though off in the distance, I could see the forest.

I pulled my phone from my bag to find out where I was. If I had to, I could haul the perishable food I'd bought on foot, though I shuddered at the thought.

My bad luck turned worse when I saw the battery had died.

"When the hell did the battery die?" I cursed, my mood growing darker as the snow got deeper. I threw my phone onto the passenger seat and twisted my keys in the ignition, hoping against hope that I would be able to start it up again. The engine made a half-hearted attempt to turn over before dying once more.

I slammed the back of my head against my seat, frustrated beyond measure. What was I supposed to do now?

Glancing outside, I noticed a house with its lights on. Maybe one of the residents would know how to fix my car. Or if I was lucky, would be willing to drive me to my mom's house. It was worth a try.

Steeling myself against the frigid air, I opened the door and rushed up the front path of the house, pausing to take a breath before ringing the doorbell.

For a few moments, nothing happened, and I wondered if the people inside were going to ignore me, but then I heard the thud of footsteps and the sound of the front door being unlocked.

"Oh, my God, I'm so sorry," I began immediately as soon as the person opened the door a crack, "but my car broke down and —Eli?"

Eli looked surprised by the sight of me on his doorstep in the middle of a snowstorm.

"Emily?" He stared at me in confusion, as if he couldn't believe I was there. "Are you okay? What were you saying—your car broke down?"

I nodded. "My phone's dead, so I had no way to ask for help or find out where I was. I figured there was no harm in trying the closest house to beg for assistance."

He looked over my shoulder at my car and frowned. "What were you doing out, anyway?"

"I went over to the next town to buy food."

"Indian Springs? That was reckless."

In hindsight, he was right, but another day of fried potatoes would have killed me outright. "I know, but I was desperate. Wilkes' stock is … not enough."

"You're telling me." He looked past me into the storm. "Any clue what's wrong with the car?"

I shook my head. "Not the slightest."

He glanced back inside his house before cursing. "All my tools are at the office. Pax needed the truck to help Lucy, and I don't think my car would be safe in this weather."

"Oh." I didn't know what else to say. I shuffled my feet. "I guess I could try the next house over."

"Don't be ridiculous," he cut in, waving the notion away. "Let's grab your groceries and put them away in my kitchen. You can stay here until the weather lets up, then I'll drive you back."

"Are you sure?"

His features softened with a smile. "Positive."

The two of us hauled the bags out of my car and into Eli's house, where he directed me to his kitchen. It was modern with granite countertops, and a six-burner stove with a stainless-steel finish.

I whistled in appreciation. "Nice kitchen, Eli."

"Thanks. Wish I could use it more right now, but I lack ingredients. I've been living on frozen pizzas."

I gasped in horror as we put the perishable things away. "That's unacceptable. You're going to get sick if you eat like that." I listed off a list of health issues that ranged from vitamin deficiency to obesity.

He laughed as he tossed a can of tomatoes into the air, catching it before it hit the countertop. "Maybe, but what else can I do? Starve?"

I glanced at the groceries strewn across his kitchen counter. "Maybe we could make dinner together? It doesn't look like I'm going anywhere for a while."

Eli's eyes lit up. "I'd love that."

I flushed from the intensity of his enthusiasm. "Would an Irish stew be okay? I've been dying to make one ever since I got to Frazier Falls"

"That sounds amazing. Do you have all the ingredients? I know a pretty great biscuit recipe."

I searched through the bags until I located the fresh produce. I had carrots and red potatoes and onions and fresh thyme. "I do. Do you mind if I use your phone to call my mom? She'll be getting worried."

"Of course not. The landline is down the hall, and there are a couple phone chargers in the drawer below it. You can see if one of those fits your cell."

He was back to rescuing me, sheltering me, saving me. He seemed to do that a lot. "Thanks."

"Don't mention it."

After assuring my mom that I was okay and telling her that there were leftovers in the fridge for her to heat up, I removed my shoes and jacket and left them by the front door, before sneaking around to find a bathroom. When I did, I used the mirror to inspect my reflection and tried to fix my hair. I risked rummaging through Eli's medicine cabinet and found a comb. I gave myself a quick brush-through before fluffing it up.

Content with the fact that I looked the best I could, given the circumstances, I wandered back to Eli's kitchen, with my heart hammering too quickly inside my chest.

The air already smelled delicious with hints of onion and spices.

He glanced up at me from the chopping board, where he was cutting up fresh carrots into bite-sized chunks. A suspicious look danced across his face. "That took a while."

I smiled bashfully. "I may have used your bathroom and your comb."

"I was wondering how your hair suddenly looked flawless." He waved me over. "Can you take over cutting the vegetables? I'll prep the lamb."

"Of course."

The next thirty minutes were filled with the sounds and smells of a kitchen in use. My stomach growled louder with every passing minute. The stew promised to be the tastiest meal I'd had in a month. I knew it would be worth the wait.

When Eli brought out a bag of flour and chopped butter into small pieces, throwing them into a bowl with salt and spices, I was curious.

"What are you making?"

"The biscuits. They're great with stew but also with white gravy and scrambled eggs for breakfast."

"Okay, color me impressed. I didn't know you went so far with your cooking."

He laughed. "I like to cook."

"Me too."

"What a happy coincidence."

Once the first batch was cooked, I couldn't help but steal one and slather it with butter and a drizzle of the honey Eli kept on the counter.

"There won't be any left for our plates at this rate," he complained, but he was grinning at me standing there with puffy, food-filled cheeks.

"These are so good. Ridiculously good, Eli. Where did you learn to make them?" I asked around a mouthful of food.

He shrugged. "My mom made them every weekend. I paid attention because there's nothing as satisfying as a biscuit straight out of the oven."

"That's a lot of effort to go to for yourself."

"Nah, my brothers like it when I cook them too. I usually make a massive batch in one shot for them to devour."

I snuck around behind him to reach the fridge; our bodies barely brushing against each other as I did. Eli stiffened immediately, and I saw his hand twitch in my direction, but then he relaxed and let it fall to his side.

Disappointment seized me. Suppressing a sigh, I rummaged through the refrigerator, looking for something wet. "Do you have anything to drink that isn't beer? Preferably alcoholic."

My breath hitched when Eli leaned over me in order to reach a well-hidden bottle of white wine.

"Will this do?" he asked, his voice a soft murmur against my ear.

My face heated like it was on fire, and I suddenly became acutely aware that I had lost my ability to speak. I nodded, not trusting my voice one bit. My heart hammered like a drum. It was strong and loud enough that I was sure Eli could hear its cadence.

When he snaked his arm around my waist, I gasped in surprise, but all he did was pull me away from the refrigerator in order to close it.

"No point in wasting the central heating by letting all that cold air out."

I turned around to look at him closely. By the pulse of the vein on his forehead, I could tell his heart was beating as quickly as mine.

"Are you nervous?" I bit out, keeping my eyes locked on his.

The creases deepened as he smiled. "Yes. Though not as nervous as you, it seems."

I let out a shaky laugh. "This is ridiculous. I feel like I'm sixteen again."

"I feel much the same way. Except sixteen-year-old me didn't know how to cook." He pulled away from me to check on the stew, which was bubbling away on the stove. "I think that's done."

He leaned back in, his face mere millimeters away from my own. I found myself holding my breath, hoping he'd kiss me.

"How about we pick this up after dinner, Flanagan?"

It was a brazen request I wholeheartedly wanted to explore. I brushed the fingers of my left hand against the side of Eli's jeans as I moved away to locate two wine glasses. I glanced back at him over my shoulder and smirked.

"Sounds like dessert to me."

CHAPTER FIFTEEN

ELI

The stew Emily and I made was one of the most satisfying meals I'd had in a long time. We didn't bother sitting at my dining room table. Instead, we curled up on the sofa to eat while half-watching an action film that was forgotten once it was finished.

We worked our way through the bottle of wine I'd found in the fridge. By the time we were full, we were also pleasantly tipsy.

My house hadn't experienced this much excitement since I'd moved in, and all we'd done was cook and eat dinner. I thought of the incredibly sexually charged moment Emily and I had shared in the kitchen as I stole a glance of her beside me. It sent a quiver down my spine, leaving me pleasantly aroused.

Below my stomach, my insides coiled and unraveled when Emily ran a hand through her fiery red hair. I wanted nothing more than to run my own hands through it. To sweep it away from her face and pin her down with it. I wanted to wrench open the buttons of her oversized flannel shirt, to—

"Eli?"

Emily looked at me with a quizzical expression.

I laughed slightly. "Sorry. What's up?"

"What are you thinking about?"

I paused, moving away from the sofa in order to prod at the fire I'd built. It needed more fuel, but I didn't have it in me to leave the warm confines of my house to get wood from the shed.

I gave Emily a mischievous smile as I sat back down beside her, then took a long drink of wine.

"I'm not entirely sure it's safe for polite conversation," I replied. A wickedly sexy thought made me smile.

Emily's eyes widened. "Now, I need to know."

I paused for a moment, considering what to say. I put down my glass and cocked my head to one side.

"Put your wine down, and I'll show you."

Emily's face flushed scarlet as she indulged my request, leaning over to the coffee table to delicately put down her glass before sitting with her back straight and her hands folded neatly in her lap.

I laughed. "What's with the overly serious posture?"

"Give me a break. I'm nervous. It's been a long time since I've indulged in this type of dessert." Emily scowled good-naturedly. "It feels like I can hardly hear anything over the sound of my own bloody heart."

"Let's start with a nibble."

My heart was pounding, too. So hard, it was almost painful.

I knew there was only one way to relieve that ache.

I closed the distance between us, gently stroking the side of her face with the back of my hand. She glanced down for half a second before her eyes flitted back to mine. She shifted closer, sliding a tentative hand over the top of my knee and halfway down my thigh. The action threatened to undo me completely.

Instead, I forced myself to keep hold of my composure. I wasn't a teen on his first date.

I slid my hand from Emily's cheek into her hair, lost in the silky softness of it.

She leaned into my touch, humming as I threaded my fingers through her tresses to pull her against my lips for a kiss.

What I wasn't expecting was for Emily to push me down onto the sofa as soon as our lips touched. Or climb on top of me to deepen the kiss as the entire length of her body moved against me.

I needed no other sign than that to carry on. My hands roved up and down Emily's body, sliding underneath her shirt to feel the heat of her skin against my fingertips. One of her legs settled between my thighs to torture me as I rushed to undo her buttons.

She ran her hands through my hair, moaning against my lips as my tongue entered her mouth, and my hands tugged her shirt free.

Squirming beneath her, I managed to remove my T-shirt. With the fabric thrown to the side, Emily's hands moved across my chest, snaking their way up, then down to my belt, making quick work of the buckle as I fumbled slightly with the clasp of her bra.

With a deft hand, she reached back and undid the clasp herself.

"Out of practice, Cooper?" she mused in a low murmur.

"Yes," I replied breathlessly. "Sit up, Emily."

She did so with a small smile on her face, allowing me to revel in the sight of her, topless and straddling me, in the dim light of the living room. The glowing embers of my dying fire reflected in her hair and eyes and painted shadows across her skin.

I ran my hands up her stomach and across her breasts, thumbs lingering on her nipples until she sucked in a breath.

"You're so beautiful," I whispered.

She looked down at me with heavy-lidded eyes.

"You're not so bad yourself."

I tore my eyes away from her to glance at the fire. It was getting down to a few red, angry embers. If I didn't tend to it soon, it would die, but there was somewhere else we could go that would be plenty warm, and altogether more comfortable than the sofa for what we were about to do. I picked her up and threw her over my shoulder as I stood, eliciting a shout of surprise.

"What are you—put me down, Eli!" she half-laughed and half-complained.

I shook my head as I made my way for the stairs, taking the opportunity to caress her ass in the process.

"Nope."

"I have two legs. I can use them."

"Sure, you can use them. In bed."

"That was filthy."

"Do you have a problem with that?"

There was a pause.

"Absolutely not."

I grinned as we reached my bedroom. I kicked the door open and dropped Emily unceremoniously onto my bed, not even bothering to turn the light on. As quickly as I could, I removed my jeans and underwear to a low, appreciative whistle from Emily.

"That's … a lot," she admitted, eyes firmly on my length. I only grew harder in response to the comment.

"Are you sure you can handle me, Flanagan? Maybe a little too much, too soon?" I murmured as I crawled on top of her, sliding my hands underneath the waistband of her leggings in order to pull them down.

She flung her arms around my neck.

"It would seem I have quite an appetite tonight."

———

I WOKE TO A DARK ROOM, the whooshing of another person's gentle breathing the only sound breaking the silence. Outside the frosty window, in the dead of night, everything was quiet. I rolled over to check the time on my phone; it was past four in the morning. One glance to my left brought a smile to my face.

Emily was sleeping soundly, hands around the top of the duvet to bring it up to her chin. She looked content and comfortable.

Once I adjusted to the dark, I left the bed and wandered over to my bathroom to grab a glass of water, pouring one for Emily, too. No doubt she'd want one when she woke up. I downed the icy cold liquid, then poured another.

When I returned, she was watching me, eyes glinting in the dark.

"Sorry." I handed her a glass of water, which she took with an appreciative smile. "I didn't mean to wake you."

"It's okay." She yawned. "I think it was the running water that woke me up. Clearly, unconscious me knew I was thirsty."

I returned to my side of the bed, sliding under the covers and lying on my side to look at her.

"You okay?" I asked, a little nervous.

She raised an eyebrow. "What does that mean?"

"Um … I don't know," I admitted. "You don't regret this or anything, do you?"

"Should I?"

"I hope not."

"Then, I sure as hell don't."

I laughed quietly. "And you're not … hurt? Everything still working okay?"

Emily smiled mischievously as she rolled over, climbing on top of me in the process.

"I don't know. Why don't we find out?"

She kissed me, long and hard, before pulling away to watch me carefully with her green eyes. They were almost glowing in the dark, making her look ethereal, like something out of a dream.

"You're definitely a real person, right?" I asked before I could stop myself. "This isn't some long, drawn-out winter fever dream I'm having, is it?"

Emily laughed softly as she kissed the tip of my nose.

"If this is a dream, let's not wake up from it for a while." Her hand snaked down my chest and stomach, lingering on the edge of my hipbone.

I wrapped my arms around her waist as I lifted up to kiss her. I felt like Emily was a human timer, and the countdown to zero, and her departure were coming all too soon.

CHAPTER SIXTEEN

EMILY

I woke with a start, a heavy arm across my chest, preventing me from moving. I turned my head to the right and found Eli fast asleep, his limbs spread out like a man who was most definitely used to having the bed to himself.

It made me giggle despite my attempt to stay silent.

I glanced out the window. Everything was quiet. No snow. No wind. No sun either.

There was no telling what time it was—it could have been nine in the morning or four in the afternoon. I rolled out of bed and gently padded from his room to the adjoining bathroom to freshen up. Under my eyes were dark smudges left from the mascara I hadn't removed the day before.

"Been a while since I've gone to bed with makeup on," I mumbled as I cleaned my face. It wasn't as if there would have been a right time to interrupt my evening with Eli in order to take it off. I suppressed a laugh as I thought about it. "Hey, Eli, care to get off me for a moment so I can wipe off my mascara? I swear it won't ruin the mood."

"Are you talking to yourself?" Eli called from the bed, causing me to flinch and grow red.

"Yes," I left the bathroom to rejoin him in bed. I suddenly felt shy without any clothes on and held the duvet up against my chest to keep myself covered. He watched me with a curious look on his face.

"There's no point in being modest after last night. The two of us indulged, like, four times."

I smiled bashfully in response; hearing the exact number of times we'd had sex last night made everything seem far more real.

"I guess not," I said. "What time is it?"

"After ten. Do you want some coffee?"

"I'd kill for it."

"No murder required." He rolled out of bed and tugged on his jeans, zipping them, but leaving the button undone. "Hang tight, and I'll make us some." While I enjoyed all views of Eli, him walking out with low slung jeans to get me coffee was pretty great.

Eli was gone for almost ten minutes, during which time I inspected his room. It was clean and organized with a large wooden dresser that no doubt held all of his clothes. On the wall by the window hung a photo of what I assumed to be his entire family from when he was a boy. I climbed out of bed, hugging the comforter around my shoulders to look closer. Owen and Eli looked like clones of their dad. Paxton stood out against them, but then I saw their mom's blond hair and understood where he'd inherited his looks.

"I bet he was a mommy's boy," I said as Eli returned with my shirt and bra hung over his arm as he carried a tray holding coffee and toast.

"Who? Paxton?" Eli asked.

I nodded.

"Absolutely. That was probably because of all the adoption jokes, though."

"You guys were awful to him, weren't you?" I smiled in thanks when I returned to the bed, and Eli handed me a cup of coffee. I inhaled the fresh aroma with a contented hum.

"He certainly makes up for it now, so it's all good."

"What, by being annoying?"

"Exactly."

We ate and drank in companionable, near-naked silence for a while, then, with a heavy sigh, I located my clothes and got dressed.

Disappointment covered Eli's face.

"Leaving so soon?"

I walked over to look out the window. The thick blanket of dark clouds promised more snow sooner rather than later.

"I think it's best for my ma if you can get me and the groceries back as soon as possible."

He joined me by the window, snaking an arm around my waist as he kissed my neck. "I can't tempt you to stay for another half-hour?"

I shook my head, though the kisses Eli planted along my collarbone begged me to reconsider. "I need to get back to look after her, and I need to work out how to fix the car."

His mouth tipped into a confident smile. "Leave that to me. I'll get my tools from the office and see what I can do. When I get it running, I'll bring it to your mom's. Does that work for you?"

"Eli, that's ... thank you. You've helped me out so much already. Is there anything I can do in return?"

He raised a suggestive brow.

"That doesn't involve getting undressed?" I added on, chuckling.

He pretended to think for a moment. "How about a date?"

"A date? Didn't we technically just have one? Albeit, accidentally."

"I mean a date somewhere else. Not in either of our houses. And not in Frazier Falls if we can manage it."

I looked out the window at the clouds, which seemed to be pressing down upon us. "I'm not sure that would be possible, given the weather."

"How about we set it for a week from now, and if the weather clears up, then great? If not, I guess we'll have to make do with getting naked in front of the fire."

I burst out laughing. "Sounds tempting." I tallied up the date in my head, then frowned at him. "A week from now is Valentine's Day."

He looked surprised. "Is it? Crap, February is flying by. We can change the date if that's too corny for you."

I smiled. "No, the date's fine." I reminded myself that I had to leave for Los Angeles a few days later so I wouldn't lose my job. It crossed my mind to turn him down. A Valentine's Day date was for lovers. Eli was … I couldn't say. He was more than a friend, but he was also temporary. That thought made my heart ache, which meant I cared for him more than I wanted to. He knew as well as I did that I had to leave. At least the date could end whatever our relationship had become on a positive note.

"Do you have anywhere in mind? For the date, I mean."

He shrugged. "I have a few ideas. Leave it to me. It's not as if you know the area well enough to plan something, anyway."

"Harsh, but true." I turned to him. It killed me to ask because he was sexy wearing a pair of jeans hanging off his hips, but I had to. "Care to get dressed and help me with the groceries? I somehow doubt you want a particular body part of yours to get frostbitten."

"That would be correct."

Fifteen minutes later, Eli drove me to my mom's house. He

helped me get the groceries to the porch, then carried them through to the kitchen after I unlocked the front door. Mom sat at the breakfast bar with a bowl of cereal and yesterday's newspaper. Her eyes lit up when she saw the two of us.

"Emily. I was getting worried." She looked at Eli. "How are you? Thank you so much for taking care of my little girl. Did the two of you have a good night?"

"That's between me and Eli, Ma," I replied, kissing her on the cheek as I began to put the groceries away.

"We did, thank you, Judy," Eli answered.

I rolled my eyes. "Kiss ass."

"I think it's great you've found yourself an honest man, sweetheart. I don't have to be worried about you if you're with him."

"You never had to worry about me when I was by myself, either."

She made a noise but otherwise didn't respond.

I filled the kettle and put it on to boil without asking if she wanted tea, since she always wanted tea.

I glanced at Eli. "Would you like some tea?"

"I'd love to stay, but I have to get to the office."

"You need to come around for dinner again," my mother added.

He glanced at me. "I guess that's up to Emily."

I hesitated for a moment, but there was no point in being coy or playing hard-to-get. "You could come tonight … you're bringing the car later, anyway. We could make enchiladas."

Eli leaned forward as if he was going to kiss me, but then thought better of it and shifted back.

"That would be great."

"I hope you're not expecting me to eat those enchi-whatevers," my mom said.

I laughed. "No, Ma. Do you want mac and cheese?"

"Oh, that sounds wonderful. Okay, go and show your man out and then make me that tea."

"Yes, ma'am," I replied sarcastically, giving Eli a push. When we reached the front door, he grabbed me, by the front of my shirt, and kissed me, hard.

I pushed him against the door in response, leaning into the kiss as much as I could. I ran a hand along the stubble of his jaw and up into his hair, pulling a low moan from his mouth against my lips.

"Stop that, Flanagan." He glanced down at his growing erection. "I can't go to the office in this state."

I smirked. "You started it."

He kissed me lightly and pushed me away. "And now, unfortunately, I have to finish it."

I rolled out my bottom lip. "And here I was thinking we could get a quickie in before you left."

"Really?" He looked conflicted for a moment.

"I was joking. Kind of. My ma wants tea, and I can't keep her waiting. What time works for dinner tonight?"

"Seven?"

"Seven works for me. I'll see you then."

After another quick kiss, he left.

I stood by the front door for a minute or so, wondering when it was going to sink in that we had slept together. Who was I kidding, sleep wasn't actually part of the equation. He'd made my body heat for him all night long.

When I returned to the kitchen, mom was fiddling with the teapot.

"What are you doing?" I rushed over to the stove. "Let me do that."

She glanced at me. "I can make a cup of tea, for goodness' sake."

I opened the lid and looked inside. There was no tea bag. It was all hot water. I suppressed a laugh as I brought out the tea bags I'd bought yesterday.

"I finally managed to get a hold of those classic tea bags you like, so no more making do with Earl Grey."

"I was starting to get fond of it, actually."

"I can make it if you'd like."

My mom's eyes widened in horror. "Absolutely not. Nothing beats a good cup of strong, English tea."

"English tea that comes from India, Sri Lanka, and Africa."

She waved a hand. "You and your silly geography."

"Yes, having a solid understanding of imports and exports is merely a silly hobby. Heaven forbid, the knowledge is useful."

"Speaking of geography," she said, ignoring my jibe. "Any update on the weather? It didn't look too bad this morning."

"I'm not sure, actually." I was immediately curious. "Let's go check on the TV."

I plopped myself down on the armrest of the sofa as I flicked through the channels, stopping when I reached a local weather station. I watched intently, taking in everything that was said, then pulled out my phone to check a few other forecasts.

"What's the consensus?" she asked.

"Seems like they think this week should be the last of the storms. A warm front is coming in from the south. That should help melt the snow."

"That's great news for you. You'll be able to get back with no worries about your job."

"Yeah ... no worries at all."

I was happy that I'd be able to finally make it back to work. Getting back to Los Angeles was all I had wanted for the past six weeks. But now, with the weather forecast telling me that I'd finally be able to leave, my stomach twisted, and my heart ached. Leaving felt ... wrong.

If the forecast was right, I'd be in California a day or two after my date with Eli, which suddenly seemed far too soon. I'd thought I'd have until the twentieth, like Don had said. The reality was that I had to get back to my job, my apartment, my friends, and my life.

It looked like my first official date with Eli Cooper would also be the last.

CHAPTER SEVENTEEN

ELI

My stomach churned non-stop from the moment I woke up. I was all frayed edges and nerves trying to make tomorrow's date with Emily perfect.

The weather had slowly but surely improved, and the snow was finally melting. That meant Emily would be leaving soon, and our first date would likely be our last.

On the upside, the end of the heavy snowfall meant that Owen and Rich finally returned to Frazier Falls. I walked the line between ecstatic and unhappy.

We were having dinner at Owen's tonight to celebrate, but as I readied myself to leave, I wished it were another day. Spending time with my family meant I wasn't spending time with Emily.

No doubt, I was acting like an idiot, worrying over the details of our date. A date that shouldn't matter because it would ultimately lead to nothing. It wasn't like I was asking Emily to marry me, or heaven forbid, move to Frazier Falls. No, it was simply an overnight stay at a hotel and spa an hour or so out of town.

Suddenly, I wanted to keep the plans for the date a surprise, which was why I hadn't told Emily to pack a bathing suit. And what if she hadn't brought one with her to Frazier Falls? Why would she in the middle of winter?

Nonetheless, I had to let her know. If she didn't have one, we'd have to find somewhere to buy one, which didn't seem likely in February. Suddenly my plan felt short-sighted and poorly executed.

I quickly pulled out my phone and called her. She picked up on the third ring.

"Eli? What's up?"

"Do you have a bathing suit?"

She hesitated for a moment before asking, "Do you mean in general, or in Frazier Falls?"

"Frazier Falls. Do you have one?"

"As a matter of fact, I do. I brought one with me in case the recreation center was open."

"It closed down two years ago."

"Yeah, I heard. Guess I wasn't ever invested enough to know that," she replied off-handedly.

"Regardless, bring it with you tomorrow."

I could almost hear her brain working, the cogs churning with every possible scenario where a swimsuit would be required. "You're not going to force me to go swimming in the creek, are you? Because I'm sure as hell not going near it."

"Why would I do that? Pack a bathing suit, and don't ask any more questions."

"Fine, but your behavior warrants my suspicion."

Like me, Emily was a storyteller, and I'm sure she'd already come up with a few potential blockbusters ranging from a polar bear dip in the creek to a jet on the nearest runway waiting to take us to a tropical island. "Just trust me. I'll pick you up at noon tomorrow."

"Fine, fine," Emily grumbled. "Tomorrow at noon with my bathing suit packed. I'll see you then."

The call ended with a click. But no sooner had I put my phone back in my pocket than it began to ring again, so back out it came. I brought the phone to my ear without checking who was calling. I had a fairly good guess, after all.

"What do you need, Owen?" I asked, looking at the clock. I was due to be at his house in five minutes. "I'm on my way."

"You can start by replacing Carla's beers that you drank," he said.

I smiled slightly at the comment. "I guess I could do that. Anything else?"

"She's asking if you can drop by Wilkes' and see if they have any cocoa powder back in stock." There was a muffled sound as if he'd placed his hand over the receiver. "What was that, Pax?" Owen's voice trailed off as our youngest brother murmured something to him. Owen sighed. "Pax wants ice cream. Feel free to ignore that, though."

"What flavor?" I asked as I pulled on my jacket. I grabbed a Tupperware container full of biscuits.

"No, seriously," Owen said, "don't indulge him. He's not a kid."

But I could hear Pax shout out 'cookie dough,' so after saying goodbye to Owen, I drove over to Wilkes'. Nobody was there except for Rachel, who sat behind the register. The store was quiet but for the incessant humming of the space heater behind the counter.

I picked up a couple of six-packs of beer and an obnoxiously large tub of ice cream—simply to annoy Owen, who would have to find space for it in his freezer, and then I headed over to Rachel to pay.

She raised a silver eyebrow. "Night in with Judy's daughter?"

Glancing down at what I was buying, I burst out laughing at

Rachel's assumption. Of course, it looked as if I was planning a night in with a girlfriend.

I shook my head. "Night in with my brothers—and Carla—hang on a second." I rushed away from the counter to look for cocoa powder. It had thankfully been restocked, which meant Carla would deem me her savior once I got to Owen's. I grabbed a box of the stuff and headed back to pay the bill. Rachel glanced at the cocoa in my hand.

"Are you sure you're not spending the night with Emily?"

"Hardly. This is for Carla."

Rachel's eyes lit up. "It's not long until her and Owen's wedding."

"It's still a while away," I reasoned. "The end of May … oh lord, that's barely three months from now."

"You might be good with numbers, Eli," she laughed as I gave her the exact change for the groceries, "but you sure are bad with dates. Have a lovely evening with your brothers."

"I can try," I called out over my shoulder as I left the store, rushing back to my car before the wind could cut through my clothes. Though the weather was letting up, it was still damn cold, and I wanted nothing more than to get back inside a warm house.

The roads were covered in an icy slurry as I carefully drove to Owen's. It made for dangerous driving, especially now that the sun had set. Everything would surely turn to ice.

It was with some relief that I made it without slipping once, though I couldn't help myself from laughing when I left my car and had to grab onto the door in order to stop from falling face-first onto the slick pavement. With care, I retrieved the groceries from the trunk and made my way to Owen's front door.

I didn't knock. I never did. We were family, so I let myself in.

"Close the door, close the door!" Pax called out. "You're letting all the heat out." He reached for the throw on the arm of the couch and covered himself.

"I guess I'll leave with this massive tub of ice cream, then."

Pax tossed off the blanket and leaped over the couch to pluck the bucket from my hands. He grinned like a kid in a candy shop as he moved to the kitchen to get a spoon.

"Thanks, bro," he said, sparing no time in tearing off the lid and digging into the frozen goodness inside. To my left, Owen let out a heaving sigh.

"Why on earth did you get him that much ice cream? I don't have enough space to store that in my freezer."

I shrugged. "Guess Pax will have to eat the whole thing, then."

"You will not do that," Owen said, firing a warning glance at Paxton. "You're thirty-two years old. You don't need to eat half a gallon of ice cream in one sitting."

"I don't need to, but I can. And besides, Eli will help me with it."

I shook my head and chuckled. "A beer's fine for me," I said as I pulled a cold one from the fridge.

Rich and Carla suddenly appeared from the study, the two of them clearly arguing good-naturedly about something or another. Rich's eyes widened when he saw the ice cream.

"Is that cookie dough?" he asked as he got a spoon from the kitchen. Pax nodded happily, his mouth full.

Rich threw himself on the sofa beside Pax and scooped out an absurdly large spoonful, saying, "Excellent," before somehow managing to fit the entire thing into his mouth.

"You're going to regret that, Rich," Carla laughed. Then she glanced at the cocoa powder I'd brought. She squealed in delight and ran over to hug me.

"Thank you, thank you, thank you!"

"Not a problem," I said before taking my beer and sitting on the floor, with my back leaning against the sofa.

Pax moved his leg as if to kick me, but I grabbed it with my right hand and fired him a warning glance. "Don't even think about it."

He swallowed the bite. "Here we are, together at last, and you're immediately picking on me."

"Who was it that bought you that ice cream you're currently inhaling?"

"Everyone knows you only did that to annoy Owen."

He had a point. "You're right, but that's beside the point."

Owen and Carla settled on the other sofa by the fireplace. Carla had her hands curled contentedly around a mug of hot chocolate, and her face held an expression of pure bliss.

"And besides," Pax said, "if there's anyone you need to be concerned about with their sugar addiction, then it's definitely Carla. She looks like a crackhead who finally got high after days of withdrawal."

"Nice one, Pax." Carla stuck her tongue out at him.

"My living room isn't big enough for this many people at once," Owen muttered as we talked over one another in easy, lazy conversation.

"It'll only get smaller if things between Eli and Emily get serious," Pax said.

Everyone's heads immediately turned to me.

"What do you want me to say?" I asked unamused. "I like her, but she'll be gone soon. Things are casual between the two of us."

"Sure, because people in a casual relationship hang out with each other every night and spend all day texting and calling, and fixing cars, and delivering them in person," Owen mused. "Yeah, definitely nothing going on."

"And you have an overnight date with her tomorrow, don't you?" Pax asked.

Carla's eyes widened. "You do? On Valentine's Day? Oh, Eli, that's sweet."

I scowled. "That was unintentional. Besides, Emily will be leaving in a few days, anyway. We're enjoying each other's company while we have it. Valentine's Day has no meaning for us." The lie tasted bitter on my tongue. Emily meant something, and a romantic sleepover on Valentine's Day amplified the feelings that were already there.

Owen didn't look convinced, but he didn't say anything.

Rich, on the other hand, removed the spoon from his mouth and said, "What is it with you guys and being staunchly against things getting serious with a woman? Owen and Carl kept their relationship secret, for God's sake."

"That was as much Carla's decision as it was mine," Owen defended, "though your point is still valid. Eli, stop lying to yourself and admit that you're hot for this woman."

I rolled my eyes. "As if it's easy."

"It literally is," he tossed back.

Everyone was still staring at me. Eventually, I threw my hands up in the air and sighed.

"Fine. I have feelings for her. A lot of feelings, and she's leaving, which sucks. Happy now?"

"Aw, Eli." Carla pouted. "That is the worst luck. At least you get to have a great day with her tomorrow. Ending things on good terms is better than nothing."

I hated the thought of ending things when everything had just begun. "Yeah, I know. It's what I've been rationalizing the whole time."

"Why aren't you planning on giving Emily such an unbelievable date that she has no choice but to stay?" Pax asked, genuinely serious.

"Because that isn't fair. She has a job she loves in a city she loves. Neither of those are here in Frazier Falls."

"You make enough to take care of her here," Pax said.

Eli laughed. "Have you met Emily. She's the last woman who would want to be beholden to a man."

"When did you mature?" Owen asked. He locked eyes with me for a moment, a flash of understanding crossing between us. Owen knew I had always been the most mature out of us brothers. He simply hadn't acknowledged it out loud before.

"Either way," Pax said, "have you discussed your feelings with her? Do the two of you know where you stand with each other?"

I paused, considering the question. "We haven't talked about it. But we know."

He dug in for another bite. "Yeah, right. If you don't talk about it, you never know for certain."

It was an interesting stance to take, and I had to admit that I was curious. If I asked Emily point-blank how deeply she felt for me, what would she say? I guess I had one final chance to find out.

CHAPTER EIGHTEEN

EMILY

When Eli called to tell me to pack a bathing suit, I was thoroughly confused. I'd thought about it all night, and now as I waited for him to pick me up, I still had no idea why one was needed. He'd been right. I didn't know enough about the area to put together a date, which meant I couldn't work out what his plan was.

He said he wanted to take me out of Frazier Falls if the weather improved. However slow it was changing, the weather had been improving day by day, which meant he was most likely taking me out of town. By now, I'd grown familiar with the area. I vowed that next time I came to visit my mom, I'd put more effort into exploring and getting to know more people. Even I had to admit, if only to myself, that Frazier Falls wasn't all that bad. In fact, I'd almost bet it would be beautiful in summer; when the trees had leaves and the crocuses peeked out of the ground after the last frost.

The airport was finally open and working on a normal schedule. However, the roads to the airport weren't in the safest condition, so I was advised not to travel if I could avoid it. Given that I actually had plans today, I didn't mind that I still couldn't get to the airport. I had to wonder if Eli hadn't asked me out on a date with a week's prior notice, would I have hung around Frazier Falls in case he had wanted to do something with me on Valentine's Day?

I shook my head in disbelief. This was getting out of hand. Whether it was going to end up being tomorrow or the day after tomorrow or the day after that, I was leaving. I was supposed to be happy, but why did I feel lousy?

The throaty growl of Eli's truck, pulling up outside my mother's house, brought me out of my thoughts. With one final inspection of my reflection in the hallway mirror, confirming that my hair was in place, my makeup was flawless, and that my clothes matched, I grabbed my bag, shouted goodbye to my mother, and left.

Eli grinned foolishly as he walked up the sidewalk to greet me.

"You're not taking your car?" I asked as I slid onto the passenger seat, giving him a quick kiss before putting on my seatbelt.

He shook his head. "Don't want to risk it with the roads. You look gorgeous, by the way."

I blushed slightly. "Thanks. You don't look too bad yourself."

That was a massive understatement. Eli's dark hair, which had grown longer than he probably usually wore it, was slicked back as if he belonged on the set of Mad Men or some other sixties period drama. He wore a soft gray turtleneck with dark jeans and leather shoes. He looked absolutely amazing.

"I wasn't aware you possessed a sense of style," I joked. "I thought it was all T-shirts and ripped jeans with you."

He laughed at the comment as he pulled out of my mother's driveway and headed down the road, leaving Frazier Falls behind. "I mean, you're not wrong. I don't get much of an opportunity to wear nice clothes given that I'm either on a construction site or locked up in the office doing the accounting. That doesn't mean I don't have nice clothes or know how to wear them."

"Guess I'll have to find excuses for you to wear nice clothes in the future, then."

We both laughed at my comment for half a second, then became abruptly aware of what I had actually said.

Idiot. Why would I say something that implied I'd be here to see him? I silently chastised myself.

The reality of our situation, and the rapidly approaching expiration date of our relationship hung over our heads, sobering the mood immediately. Eli drove the truck in silence for ten minutes or so, the two of us struggling to find something new to talk about that would destroy the awkwardness hanging between us.

Eventually, I said, "So Owen and Rich are finally back, huh? That must be pretty great."

"Pretty annoying, that's what it is."

"You can't mean that."

Eli let out a bark of laughter. "You're an only child, aren't you?"

"Yes."

"You wouldn't get it, which is fine. Having siblings is the epitome of a love/hate relationship. I'm glad the two of them are back, but at the same time, I could have easily been happy with them staying away for another day, or a week, or a month."

"That sounds like a bit of an exaggeration."

"Possibly." He glanced at me with a smirk on his face. "Of course, I'm happy they're back, but it does mean I have two extra people grilling me about you every day."

I twisted in my seat to face him. "Is that so? And, tell me, what have they been saying?"

"Just that I better lock you down while you're still here."

That phrasing always made me laugh. My active imagination

took me many places from a padlocked cell to Mr. Grey's red room of pain. "That sounds ominous. You're not carting me off to your super scary sex dungeon, are you?"

He quirked a brow. "Why? Would you like that?"

"No…" A silly giggle bubbled up. "Probably?"

"Probably with a question mark at the end?"

"I suppose it would depend on the circumstances." I grinned wickedly.

The rest of the drive to wherever Eli was taking me, passed by like this, the two of us flirting outrageously and not touching upon the matter of what would happen once I left Frazier Falls.

When Eli parked the truck in front of an immaculate, beautiful, old-fashioned hotel, I smiled.

"This place looks lovely."

"Wait until you see the inside … and the outside."

"Okay, now I'm definitely intrigued."

He pulled our bags from the second-row seat and led me to the entrance, holding the door open for me to walk through.

"Such a gentleman."

"I have been aspiring to hear you say that since we met," he joked.

When we reached the reception desk, a well-dressed woman smiled warmly at the two of us. She reached and shook Eli's hand.

"You must be Mr. Cooper," she said. "I'm Nina, the manager of the Ruxin Hotel and Spa."

Eli frowned. "How did you know who I was?"

She smiled bashfully. "Normally, especially on Valentine's Day, the hotel would be fully booked, but with the horrible weather, and the fact Valentine's Day landed on a Wednesday this year, we're fairly quiet. You were the last guest that needed to check in."

"I suppose that works in our favor," Eli responded.

I glanced at Nina. "Did you say hotel and spa?"

Nina nodded. "I'm assuming this is your first visit?"

Giddiness danced through me. "Yes."

"They have Japanese-style outdoor baths," Eli said as he looked at me. "The reason you needed a bathing suit. Better than me throwing you in the creek, right?"

"Oh, barely," I teased, feeling my insides fire up with excitement at the idea of a heated bath and a spa. "Eli, you certainly know how to plan an excellent date."

"Don't get used to it," he murmured as we were handed our room key. We made our way into the elevator and up to the third floor. The smell of lavender scented the air. "This was the one great idea I'm likely to ever have on the subject."

It turned out Eli had booked the best room in the hotel. There was a large balcony which overlooked the beautifully landscaped grounds. Steam curled up through the air from the outdoor baths, smelling of eucalyptus and sandalwood. My muscles turned soft at the mere thought of soaking in them.

"If this is the only good date idea you ever have, then that's okay," I said, knowing this was likely the only date we would have. I fell onto the enormously large bed. It was beyond comfortable. Potentially the best bed I'd ever fallen onto.

Eli picked up two white, fluffy robes. "Feel like hitting the spa? Or are you hungry? I have the restaurant downstairs booked for dinner later, but we could always—"

"Definitely the spa first," I cut in. "Lord knows I need it."

I threw off my clothes and put on my bathing suit so quickly that Eli burst out laughing. "That's the fastest I've ever seen you undress," he chuckled. "Had I known taking you to a spa was all I needed to get you naked, I'd have suggested it the first time I saw you."

"Such a comedian."

Eli had booked the two of us for several treatments, including full-body massages and facials. We whiled away the afternoon being pampered and spoiled before relaxing in the steam rooms and going for a swim in the large outdoor pool. I kept eyeing the outdoor baths, but Eli shook his head.

"Leave that for after dinner."

"But they're calling me. Why can't we use them now?" I rolled out my lip and gave him my best pout.

He shook his head in resignation. "I may have booked one of them for private use at nine, but you had to ruin the surprise with your impatience."

I hugged him tightly, startling the other couple who was sitting in the sauna with us. "This is definitely the best date I've ever been on." I lifted my lips to give him a quick kiss. "Thank you."

"You're welcome. Thanks for being my date."

I didn't have to blush. The woman across from me did enough of it for both of us. Then she gave the man she was with a solid slug to the arm. "See that, Harold? That's what love looks like."

After hours spent in the spa, I was tempted to take a nap. I was relaxed, but I shook the sleepiness away in order to get ready for dinner. I slipped on a clingy, dark green dress that I knew Eli would love and looked in the mirror. Who was this woman who looked back at me? I was glowing with happiness, and I had that newfound love look in my eyes. I twisted my hair up, keeping a few errant strands down to frame my face and finished getting ready with red lipstick and dark mascara.

"Wow. Just ... wow," Eli exclaimed when he saw me. He wore the same clothes as before, but considering how good they looked on him, and the fact that they were already dressy, the two of us looked perfectly matched for dinner.

I sauntered over to him and planted a kiss on his lips. "Wait until you see what I'm wearing underneath," I whispered.

"Are you going to wear it in the outdoor bath?"

"Hardly. But I'm sure we can fit in a quickie between dinner and soaking."

"Oh, I like the sound of that."

Dinner was wonderful. The restaurant was nearly empty, so the service was attentive and impeccable. We enjoyed a five-course tasting menu along with champagne while we listened to the sounds of the massive, crackling fire in the restaurant's fireplace, and the gentle piano music floating through the air.

The entire time, Eli's hand stroked the side of my leg beneath the table, wandering up dangerously high when he was sure no one was looking. He grazed his hand over mine whenever I moved, twisting our fingers together while staring at me with hooded eyes. His seductive looks were setting me ablaze.

By the time we stumbled back to our room, tipsy and full and aroused, it was all we could do to unlock the door before he removed my dress, revealing the black, lacy, barely-there lingerie I wore.

"What were you hoping for when you brought this with you to visit your sick mom in Frazier Falls?" he asked as he kissed my neck, his fingers skimming underneath the lace of my panties.

"Hey, a girl can never be too prepared, and clearly, I was right to bring it along."

"Damn straight."

The lingerie didn't stay on for long. Eli seemed to ravish me as he took it off, making sure that no part of my body was left unexplored by his mouth and hands. By the time his lips finally found mine again, I was moaning in desperation.

"Eli, this was supposed to be a quickie." My words escaped on a moan. "We're going to miss the outdoor bath you booked."

He flashed his pearly whites at me. "Trust me. I'm not going to last long with you like this. We'll make the reservation. Let me have my fun."

He stuck to his guns and continued to tease me, gently biting at my breasts as his hand moved between my legs. My breath caught, and my heart raced. Eli's hair felt glorious between my fingers. I dropped my hands and clung to his back.

"For the love of God," I whimpered. "Please hurry."

He chuckled. "If that's what you want, then ..."

With a single firm thrust, Eli was inside me. He was true to his word. He didn't last long, but for the time we were connected, he was desperate and passionate and wild.

When we finished, the two of us could barely catch a breath. Eli picked me up and gingerly put me on my feet before wrapping me up in one of the fluffy robes.

"Now, it's time for the bath."

I eyed him warily, still struggling to regain my composure after what he'd done to me. "I don't have my bathing suit on, and neither do you."

He grinned as he threw a robe on himself.

"I like you naked."

CHAPTER NINETEEN

ELI

Emily and I basked in the kind of fuzzy, satisfied glow you could only get from staying up all night in bed with someone you were crazy about. Even now, driving back to Frazier Falls in the pale morning sunlight, all I had to do was look at her, and I was filled with an insatiable desire to pull to the side of the road and undress her once more.

"What are you thinking about?" she asked, a curious expression on her face.

I cocked my head to one side and raised a suggestive eyebrow, satisfied to see Emily's face blush because she knew what was on my mind.

"I'm remembering the outdoor bath," I finally said. "I wish we were back there."

"Oh, you do, do you? It seemed to me like you couldn't handle the heat for all that long."

I laughed. "Champagne and hot water are a dangerous mix. With that winter air on our faces, and with you having nothing on …" I sighed dramatically. "I almost wish we could live there."

"Almost?"

"I doubt we could sleep in water without the risk of drowning."

"That's the only issue you see with living in an outdoor bath?"

There were all kinds of problems with the concept, but it was my fantasy, and I was going with it. Anywhere I could have Emily on demand was a place I'd want to be.

"Your skin would get wrinkled, too, and wrinkling your soft skin would be a crime."

"Oh, that's terrible," she replied. "Definitely not an option."

"Definitely."

"Do you have to work this afternoon, Eli?"

Taking my eyes from the road for a second to look at her, I answered, "No. Why?"

"I thought that we could maybe ... I don't know ... extend the date a little longer in your bedroom?"

A small, excited smile curled my lips. "I like the sound of that. We could make pizza. A real one this time, from scratch."

"No frozen ingredients in sight?"

"None."

"Then it's a date."

Satisfied with the direction my day was going, I tightened my grip on the steering wheel and continued toward Frazier Falls. Who knew we'd get two dates out of one?

Emily was fiddling around with the radio stations when a phone buzzed.

"Is that mine or yours?" I asked, not taking my eyes off the road.

"Oh—it's mine. Excuse me for a minute," she said as she pulled her phone from her purse. She accepted the call and covered the phone long enough to tell me,—"it's my boss,"—before turning away to have the conversation as privately as possible.

I tried my hardest not to listen, but within the confines of the truck, and bearing in mind that Emily hadn't chosen a radio station, I could hear everything her boss was saying as clearly as if I were having the conversation with the man myself.

"Emily, I've got news," he said.

"Morning Don, great to hear from you. How are you?" Emily said in a sweet voice that told me the two of them got along well.

"I thought you'd be done with pleasantries and small talk by now, given how much Frazier Falls has grated on your nerves."

Emily glanced at me before letting out a small, uncomfortable laugh. "I'm not at rock-bottom yet. What's this news?"

"Pete's pushing for you to come back. His words were now or never. I figured now was better than unemployed. I was able to book you a flight out today. It's the only one I could get with all the cancellations and delays. It leaves at five. Can you make it?"

I risked a look at her only to see her eyes light up right before they dulled.

My mood slumped immediately. I knew what Emily was doing. She was trying to act like this wasn't the best news she'd heard in weeks.

"No, that's great, Don, I can make that. Send me the details?"

"Already have. You can take tomorrow to organize yourself, but you need to be here Monday to discuss everything about that Green House Project you sent the information about."

Her tone lifted as if she were happy. "That's wonderful. I think we can do something with it this time. Especially now that they've gained international clients."

For a brief second, we exchanged looks. I tried to keep mine neutral. On the outside, I was calm and accommodating. Inside, I was a mess of jumbled feelings that ranged from hurt to anger. On the steering wheel, my hands clenched so tightly that my knuckles turned white.

After saying goodbye, Emily ended the call, leaving a heavy

cloud of silence hanging over us. All of that wonderful, sunny atmosphere we'd cultivated during the last twenty-four hours was gone. It was as if it had never existed.

"I guess our plans are canceled."

Emily reached over to touch my arm. "Eli—"

I shrugged my arm away. "No, it's fine. I always knew you'd leave. I didn't realize it was going to be today."

"It's not like there was anything I could have done."

I couldn't help but roll my eyes, but immediately regretted it.

Emily grumbled. "What was that all about?"

"What was what?"

"Don't act childish. Why did you roll your eyes? Are you implying there was something I could have done differently?"

I had to finish what I'd inadvertently started. Pax said we needed to talk it out. Let's see how brutally wrong he was.

"Don asked if you could make that flight. You could have asked him to move it to tomorrow. You actually had plans with me."

"Are you serious?"

"He booked a flight without consulting you first. It would be reasonable for you to have had plans. Which you do."

"Which I did. Eli, I've been trying to leave for weeks. I have a job to do." She shook her head. "You want me to miss that plane because we made plans to stay in and make pizza? Is that what you're saying?"

"When you put it like that …"

"When I put it like what?"

I resisted the urge to raise my voice. I already knew this would be a fruitless argument, but now that we had started it, I found that I couldn't stop.

"Why are you willingly tossing away what we have together?"

She paused as I struggled to keep my eyes on the road. "Excuse me?" she uttered softly.

"You sound like you did on the evening we met. Is 'excuse me' all you can say to a question you don't want to answer?"

"Who are you to say that I'm willingly tossing away what we have? What do we even have in the first place? We knew what this was."

"Tell me then, what was it?" I hated that my voice had reached levels of agitation that made my words echo in the small space.

"Temporary," she burst out. "Or have you turned this into something it's not in your head—maybe another one of your stories? I always knew this would end when I left Frazier Falls, and so did you. If you suggest otherwise, then you're flat-out lying to yourself!"

"Damn it, Emily!" I pounded on the steering wheel and slammed on the brakes, screeching to a halt a couple of streets away from where Emily's mother lived. I turned around to face her, my heart beating way too fast to continue driving.

"Damn me what, Eli? This was always the scenario." Emily's voice was like thunder, echoing through my soul.

I shook my head in frustration. "Why are you lying? Why are you making this out like what we had was nothing? Is it to make leaving me easier? There's no way in hell that what's been going on between us is casual." I shook my head. "No way. I can't believe that."

"You can believe what you want, but that doesn't make it different. I have to go."

Emily turned from me to wrench the passenger door open. I grabbed onto her arm to prevent her from leaving.

The glare she threw at me could have cut through steel. "Let me go, Eli."

"No."

Her eyes widened in disbelief. "I'm telling you to let me go."

"Not until you're honest with me."

"I'm being honest with you!" she screamed, angry tears filling her eyes as she tried to pull away.

"No, you're not!"

"Stop telling me what I think."

"Then stop lying!"

"Eli." The fight in her voice was gone. "Please let me go before you ruin everything."

I laughed bitterly. "How can I ruin something that you claim doesn't exist? According to you, it was all in my head."

"Don't do this. Don't. You're asking me to choose, and I can't. Just let me go." She stared at me with pleading eyes.

As much as I wanted to keep her, I knew I couldn't, so I let her go.

Emily got out of the truck and grabbed her bag. I dug my fingernails into the steering wheel, breathing heavily with my eyes closed. Then I turned off the engine and left the truck to follow after her as she made her way down the street.

"Emily, wait," I called out. She spared an angry glance over her shoulder, then hurried forward. "You're making this so much harder."

"What else would you have me do?" She turned to face me so quickly that she slipped on the ice that lined the concrete.

I reached out to steady her. "All I'm asking is for you to admit that we were more. It would be nice if you could give me a kiss goodbye."

"Are you trying to torture me?"

We stared at each other; our faces hot and red from arguing, while our breath clouded up the air in front of us. We had come to a resolute stand-still.

The way I felt for Emily went deeper than liking her. I was certain she more than liked me back, but she didn't want to admit it because she was going to leave, regardless.

When it came down to it, if she asked me, instead, to move to Los Angeles with her, I wouldn't be able to do it. I couldn't. And that was what did it for me. It was unfair of me to try to force her to stay.

I took a few steps back. Her eyes widened slightly as if she hadn't expected me to give up so easily. What she didn't know was this wasn't easy at all.

"You're right," I said, as slowly and as calmly as I could. "There's nothing else to say. I shouldn't have said anything in the first place."

"Eli…"

"Have a safe flight home," I turned away and walked back to my truck as quickly as I could. My hands trembled as I opened the door. I fumbled with the key and dropped it twice before I shoved it into the ignition and started the engine.

When I looked up, Emily Flanagan was gone.

CHAPTER TWENTY

EMILY

"Good work today, team," Don said.

"Easy for you to say. You had a working lunch that lasted all afternoon," I tossed out.

"True, but the food was awful, and the company was worse. I'd go so far as to say my afternoon was more torturous than yours."

Sadie leaned back in her chair and clucked her tongue in response. Her head shook in sync with the sound.

Don turned to her. "Just be happy I'm not making either of you work overtime."

"There's nothing that would require overtime. Emily and I are efficient and work well together," Sadie glanced at her. "Can you believe Pete would consider breaking up the A-team?"

I arrived back at work weeks ago to a raging Pete, complaining about hiring people that never worked. He was halfway to telling me I was fired when I handed him a packet of information I'd compiled about the Green House Project.

"No chance of that happening now that we're on board with

the Cooper brothers. It's even sweeter that Emily has a connection."

I wasn't listening to the conversation until the Green House Project was mentioned. Almost a month had passed since I'd left Frazier Falls in a wave of anger and grief. I didn't want to acknowledge the heartache, but four weeks later, I was finally able to accept the fact that I'd been truly upset about leaving no matter how I tried to convince myself otherwise.

It had been so easy to lie to myself, and I was furious at Eli for everything he'd dared to say out loud. We weren't supposed to say anything even vaguely truthful. We were supposed to go on having fun, spending time with each other right until the last moment I spent in Frazier Falls.

But Eli ruined all of that by forcing me to face my feelings. I'd told myself a dozen stories. He was a pleasant distraction. We used each other to fill the boring gaps in our lives. We had nothing in common but sex. But that wasn't true.

I convinced myself that he'd been more involved than me. The relationship had been in his town, in his stores and cafes, and in his house. That was another lie. I missed my mother's hugs. I missed Alice's pie. Hell, I missed Eli Cooper with every breath I took. While I tried to convince myself that he was no one to me, he occupied all my thoughts. Today, I'd even accidentally named a park after him. Smack dab in the middle of Culver City would be Cooper Park instead of Copper Park.

Had I made the biggest mistake of my life when I left? The answer was a sorrowful no. I couldn't have it all. The job market in Frazier Falls wasn't ideal for a girl with a geography degree, and a penchant for city planning. Neither Ma nor I were fond of hunger. And another epic storm without a back-up generator wouldn't be good. I wasn't forsaking Eli—I had to choose my mother. Eli would survive if I left, but my mom might not survive if I stayed. My love for her tied me to California and a job that seemed less appealing each day.

God, this was so messed up. I couldn't believe I was sitting here at my desk, in a job I once loved, in a city I once loved, surrounded by people I still loved, and yet, I was miserably unhappy because the two people I loved the most were in Colorado.

Oh. My. God. I loved him.

"Flanagan? Emily Flanagan, hello?" Sadie waved her hand in front of my face.

I blinked before slowly turning around to see Sadie and Don looking at me with puzzled expressions.

I gave them a smile that ended up being more of a grimace.

"Sorry, I was daydreaming."

"Must have been a pretty shitty daydream," Sadie said. "Can you have a daymare? That sounds weird."

"Something on your mind, Emily?" Don asked kindly.

"Um, not really. Sort of. Yeah."

"That's one hell of a confused answer," he said.

I turned to my computer and pulled up the project details that I'd been working on. "Take a look at this."

He moved behind my chair and scanned the screen in front of him, then looked at me. "This is pretty thorough. Where did you get the time to construct this?"

"By not sleeping," I joked, even though it was true. I hadn't slept a full night in weeks.

"That explains why you haven't gone out for drinks the past couple of times, either," Sadie grumbled.

I ignored her. "Owen Cooper's Green House Project, as it stands, is built around the idea of constructing brand new, affordable, ecologically friendly houses, which is wonderful, but…"

Don frowned. "But?"

"Building from scratch every time isn't something that will work in most environments. But if we were to, how should I put it, shrink Cooper's idea in order to implement parts of his eco-friendly designs into existing houses and apartment buildings, then that might be a more effective strategy toward creating environmentally friendly homes in urban areas using what we already have. I was thinking—"

"There's even more to this scheme of yours?"

I smiled weakly. "When is there not more?"

"You're right. Continue."

I pointed to a few schematics in my plan. "The idea came to me when I was working on those park specifications. There's no reason why we can't incorporate these ideas into the green spaces we have. It would be great for the parks we're planning in the future. There's the possibility of building entire Green House neighborhoods. If we constructed mini-wind farms or park-based solar panels which local, low-income housing was connected to, then we'd effectively set up a social energy grid which would simultaneously power local residences using green energy, and also help with the financial burden of rising energy prices for the residents. On top of that, having communal energy stores would be useful if abnormal weather hit, causing the national grid to go down."

Of course, I was thinking about how my mom was left in the lurch whenever her power went out. Half of the inspiration for this entire project came from her, and my desire to fix her problem.

Don was silent for a few moments, which I knew was a good sign. It meant he was seriously considering my proposal. Eventually, he grinned.

"I like this a lot. It could do with a little more refining, and possibly a trial-run somewhere smaller, but I like it."

I grinned back. I had barely slept as I worked on this plan. It had acted as an excellent distraction from the rest of my problems. Now that I had Don's approval, I would have to get in contact with Owen Cooper or Carla Stevenson to go over my proposal with them. That filled me with excitement and dread.

What would Eli have told them about the way I broke things off? There was a reasonable chance that my prospective business partners would consider me an awful and unreliable person.

And yet, something told me that Eli, despite the way things ended, wouldn't do that to me. He was as judgmental as I was, and had an opinion about every person he met, but he was a reasonable man beneath the sarcastic comments and catty remarks.

My heart hurt thinking about him because there were so many good things about him.

Sadly, he hadn't contacted me once since I left, which I both expected and deserved. It wasn't as if I had contacted him, either. Outside of my daily check-ins with mom, everything related to Frazier Falls made my heart hurt, so I avoided it.

I thought back to the day I'd left. Mom had been upset when I rushed into the house to pack my belongings. She didn't want me to leave—not out of selfishness for her, but for a chance there might be an Eli and me.

"I take it you don't want to go out for drinks?" Sadie asked, pulling me out of my thoughts once more. "You know, the best way to get over someone is to get under someone else."

I stared at her. "Sex isn't a solution."

"Sure it is. Eli Cooper isn't the only man in the world for you."

I refused to tell her how wrong she was. "I'm exhausted. I think I'll throw myself into bed as soon as I get home."

"Sounds healthy." She looked me up and down. "You do look like hell."

"Ouch."

"Only telling it like it is. Take care of yourself this weekend."

"You too, Sadie." She turned and left the office, leaving only Don and me. I stared at him. "I thought you were leaving."

He laughed lightly. "Not before you. As in, leave now. Go to bed, like you said you were planning. You need rest."

"What are you, my dad?"

"If that's what it takes to get you to look after yourself, then sure, why not?"

"You're thirty years too young to be my dad, and he's a dead-beat son of a bitch currently living in an alcoholic stupor in the middle of nowhere, Ireland."

"Then clearly you need a stand in."

It was impossible to be in a bad mood when Don was around. He put a hand on my shoulder and squeezed slightly.

"Come on. I'll take you home."

I didn't have it in me to protest, so I shut down my computer, collected my things, and followed Don to his car. I only lived a short walk from the office, but the drive back to my apartment was appreciated once it sunk in how tired I was.

"Don't work yourself so hard," he said, pulling in front of my apartment. "Burnout won't do any of us much good."

"I know, I know. I can do better than this."

He smiled. "Everyone is allowed to have a moment or two."

Whatever song that had been playing on the radio had finished, and the DJ was giving a weather report.

Something about a major storm hitting the southwestern states, including Colorado. I tuned in to hear them say that experts were warning residents to stay indoors and prepare for potential blackouts.

"Oh, crap," I let out as my insides went cold.

His expression grew serious once he saw the look on my face. "Emily, it'll be okay. Colorado has had a month of reasonable weather. There's no snow or ice on the ground to make things dangerous. As long as your mom stays indoors, the storm will pass, and she'll be fine."

"Yeah, I guess so …" I mumbled, not entirely convinced. I couldn't shake the feeling that something was going to go horribly wrong. I chalked it up to a daughter's natural inclination to worry about her mom. I gave Don a halfhearted smile and a wave as I walked toward my apartment. "I'll see you on Monday. Have a great weekend."

"You, too. Get some sleep and stop worrying."

When I got into my apartment, I took out my phone and called mom to make sure she was okay. When she didn't pick up, I glanced at the time. It was just after six in the evening. Remembering that she was supposed to be going to Lucy Rogers' place for dinner, I forced myself to remain calm.

"She's fine," I told myself. "Go to bed early, and in the morning, everything will be okay."

Hours later, and I hadn't slept a wink. I laid on my bed, restlessly tossing and turning as sleep evaded me.

I grabbed my phone and called my mom again. I would have expected her to call me back by now, especially if she was stuck indoors by herself.

Once again, she didn't pick up. The cell phone rang until I reached her voicemail. I tried the house phone a few times for good measure in case she was asleep, but every call went unanswered.

"I'm allowed to be worried now, right?" I asked myself aloud, shivering despite the warmth of my apartment.

I didn't know what to do. If my mom didn't pick up, then I

wouldn't know what was going on. I stupidly didn't have the contact information of her friends in Frazier Falls. I had no way of reaching them to check in on her.

Then I glanced at my phone. I scrolled through my contact list as dread washed over me. I had one person who could check on her—Eli.

CHAPTER TWENTY-ONE

ELI

There was nothing like working up a sweat. Hard work and muscle fatigue satisfied in a way that office work never could.

Owen might have been inclined to disagree on the latter point, but for me, working with my hands gave me a true feeling of completion.

With the weather having cleared up over the past few weeks, Cooper Construction had finally been able to pick up the delayed February projects. We'd been working around the clock to make up for lost time, and now, in mid-March, we finally had.

The long, exhausting days were exactly what I needed to keep my mind focused on anything other than Emily Flanagan.

Finally, the snow, ice, and gale-force winds had dissipated, which meant I was never trapped inside my house with only thoughts of her for company. I managed to stop thinking about her until the end of the day when I was in bed and waiting for sleep to wash over me.

I'd never thought of my bed as too big ... until now. In a short time, I'd grown accustomed to her lying by my side, nestled against my arm or leaning on my back, her soft, slow breaths tickling my skin. It had been a wonderful experience, and I missed it more than I could bear.

My brothers, as well as Carla and Rich, knew that Emily had left quickly, but I hadn't said a word to any of them about what had transpired. What could I say? At the end of the day, Emily went back to Los Angeles at the first given opportunity, which is what she had always said she would do.

Maybe she'd been right. Maybe I had been reading too much into our relationship. Even if she had developed serious feelings for me, which a desperate part of me was clinging to as true, that didn't change a damn thing. Emily lived in Los Angeles. Her whole life was there.

And yet, knowing that she wouldn't choose me, no matter how she felt, absolutely sucked. Not for the first time since she'd left, I wondered whether it would have been such an outlandish idea for me to move to California. People always needed accountants and builders. There was no doubt I could find a job, but that went against everything I'd wanted in life.

Here in Frazier Falls, I was my own boss. I worked with people I cared about, in a town I loved. I couldn't give that up, even as part of me screamed that I should get on the next flight to Los Angeles and show up on Emily's doorstep, begging her to give us another shot.

I shook my head, laughing bitterly. All I had to do was give her a second, and she consumed my thoughts.

Out of the corner of my eye, I spotted Pax looking at me strangely.

"You finally losing it, Eli? You sound like a villain coming up with some heinous plot all by himself."

"That's a colorful imagination you have there. Get back to work."

He pointed upwards to the sky. "I don't like the look of those clouds. The wind's picking up and the temperature is dropping. I say we pack up for the day."

"Surprisingly, I agree with you," Owen said as he wandered over with Pax. "I checked the forecast. Turns out, there's a storm coming our way."

Pax looked at me suspiciously. "This wasn't your doing, was it, Mr. Villain?"

I gave him the finger.

"In any case, it's best to get the site secured against the storm," Owen directed. "Want to come to my house for a beer afterward?"

"Sounds great." Pax was always up for free beer.

I shook my head. "To be honest, these late nights are wearing on me. I think I need to get some sleep. I'll head home."

"Eli?"

"You guys go on and have fun," I pushed. "I'll join you next time."

"That's what you said last Friday," Pax said.

"And the week before," Owen added.

"And the—" Pax piped in again.

"Okay, I get it. I get it. Fine, I'll join you for one, then I'm going home."

Paxton brightened up immediately. "That's the spirit."

Owen watched me with an unreadable expression. He turned to Pax. "Why don't you stop by Wilkes' while Eli and I finish up here?"

"Don't need to tell me twice. I'm out of here," Pax said, giving Owen a mocking half-salute before hurrying off before he could change his mind.

Owen and I cleaned up the construction site in uncomfortable silence. Eventually, it grew too much for me, so I turned on him. "Spit it out, Owen."

He feigned ignorance. "Spit what out?"

"All this silent judgment you're throwing my way. Say what you want to say."

"What, that I think you're being stupid by not trying to make amends with Emily? I'm not thinking that at all."

"You're hilarious."

"Eli," Owen said, growing serious. "None of us have seen you like this before. You're barely sleeping. You're not socializing. Hell, you hardly speak a word to anybody. We're considering calling you Paxton. It's so unlike you. Of course, we're all worried."

"What, and you're so perfect?" I said, glaring at him. "I do recall a certain somebody having a panic attack on stage instead of apologizing to Carla Stevenson and getting her to help you once more."

"But that's exactly my point." Owen bundled the rest of our tools into the truck before we jumped inside and headed out. "Everything between Carla and me could have been solved if we simply communicated with each other. There was nothing else to it. Now it seems so stupid to think back on it. It seemed so complex and infuriating and impossible at the time, but in reality, it wasn't like that at all. We loved each other. What more was there to it than that?"

I made a face as a smattering of rain began to hit the windshield. "It's so easy for you to say."

Owen frowned. "What do you mean?"

"You and Carla both love Frazier Falls. There was nothing standing in the way of you guys being together. Even if the Stevenson Mill had been forced to close, Carla still wanted to live here. The two of you could have made it work no matter the outcome of your presentation."

"I wouldn't exactly say that," Owen replied, grimacing slightly.

"I know my flaws. I wouldn't have been able to face her, knowing that I had failed. Knowing that I was the reason her family business had to close. I highly doubt we'd still be together if that had happened."

I couldn't help but laugh. "Somehow, I have trouble believing that. The way you guys look at each other." I shook my head. "No way would you be able to stay away from each other."

"You think you and Emily are different?"

I paused. "You never saw us together, so how can you say anything on the matter?"

"I don't need to have seen the two of you together to know what's going on. All I need to see is you without her."

"She wants to live in Los Angeles. I want to live here. She hates Frazier Falls. What more is there to say? There's no compromise there."

Owen sighed. "Are you sure you're both not confusing want with need?"

"What do you mean?"

"Does she really love Los Angeles or simply what it gives her?"

"I'll never know."

"You could have asked her. Why didn't you?"

"I tried to talk to her. I tried to stop her, but she begged me to let her go."

"You messed up."

"Excuse me?" I almost laughed at the irony of saying those two indignant words. I sounded just like Emily.

Owen rolled his eyes. "I bet you went about it the wrong way."

"What makes you say that?"

"Because I know you. And you're an idiot. All of us brothers are."

"What, and now you have a fiancée, so you're somehow less of one?"

Owen pulled up outside the office, cutting the engine before giving me a level stare. "I'm probably no less an idiot than I was before, but now I have someone to balance me out."

I winced as the rain suddenly grew heavier, followed by a sharp gust of wind that rocked the truck.

"Maybe we could continue this lecture somewhere else, or, you know, stop having it altogether."

Owen laughed. "Sounds like a plan, but think about what I've said. Now get out. I'll see you at the house in a few."

I glanced over at my own truck, then up at the sky. "I'm only staying for one beer."

"One to start."

"I'm afraid not."

"I thought I was the one getting old."

"Getting old and being sensible are two different things."

"Debatable."

I followed Owen out of the parking lot, then made my way through the torrential rain to his house. When we got there, Pax was already inside building a fire.

"Thanks for that," Owen said.

We enjoyed the fire. I made everyone dinner and nursed my one beer while my brothers moved onto their fifth. By the time it hit nine, I was thoroughly exhausted and dreaming of bed. The wind roared outside while the rain pelted against the windows like bullets.

"Owen, did we move over to the backup generator in the past few hours?" Pax asked nonchalantly. "The lights haven't flickered at all."

"I actually swapped over to it as soon as we got in," he explained. "Figured a blackout was inevitable, so I thought I'd play it safe."

I frowned. "The power went out?"

"Nearly two hours ago, I think." He searched through his phone for a weather update. "Yeah, after seven. Why?"

"No reason." An uneasy feeling knotted in my stomach, and I didn't know why. Just then, my phone vibrated in my pocket. I took it out to see Emily's name flash across my screen.

I nearly didn't answer. I didn't know what I would say, but something told me I had to pick up.

"Odd hearing from—"

"Eli, please," Emily cut through, not letting me speak. Her voice sounded panicked and desperate, which immediately set me on alert.

"What is it, Emily?" All thoughts about being angry, or dismissive, or insulting went out the window. Out of the corner of my eye, I saw my brothers watch me with interest, having heard me utter Emily's name.

"It's my mom," she answered. "She hasn't—she won't pick up the phone."

"How long have you been trying to contact her?"

"Since six. She's not answering the house phone or her cell. Eli, I don't know what to do. Is the power out?"

"Yes, for a couple of hours. That's probably why you can't get her on the house phone." I tossed my empty bottle into the trash can. "You want me to check on her?"

"Could you please?"

Her voice was scratchy and frantic and full of tears. All I wanted to do was hold her tightly against my chest. How was I ever angry at her?

"You bet," I replied, grabbing my jacket and moving toward the front door without so much as a goodbye to my brothers. I threw myself into my truck and started up the engine, balancing my phone between my ear and my shoulder as I pulled out of Owen's driveway. "Emily, it'll be okay. Hang tight, and I'll call you back as soon as I get to your mom's place, okay?"

"Thank you." The words were barely audible. "Thank you, Eli, thank you. I don't—"

"Don't say anything," I interrupted. "There'll be time for talk later. Look after yourself, and I'll call soon."

I hung up before Emily could say any more. The horrific storm outside forced me to keep my full attention on the road in front of me. It took an agonizingly long time to reach Judy's house, but when I did, my heart went cold.

Judy's car was in the driveway, but all her lights were off. The house was silent.

I'd barely pulled to a stop before I flung myself out of the driver's seat, slamming open Judy's door once I twisted the handle and found it unlocked.

In the darkness, I called her name. "Judy? Ms. Flanagan? Are you awake?"

I walked through the living room first and found her lying on the floor in front of the sofa. Clearly, she'd rolled off of it to the hardwood floor. I knelt down by her side, checking her pulse. Her skin was cold to the touch. My hands trembled, but underneath my fingertips, I could feel her life beating against my skin.

I shook Judy's shoulders. "Judy, wake up. Judy?"

But she didn't wake up. She continued to lay there, unconscious and unresponsive.

I grabbed the blanket off the sofa and bundled her in it, then carefully carried her out to my car. I cranked up the heat and raced to the hospital.

"Hold on, Judy," I murmured aloud, as much for me as for her. "Hold on. You can do this."

I didn't want to think about what would happen if she couldn't.

CHAPTER TWENTY-TWO

EMILY

It felt like a lifetime had passed waiting by my phone for Eli to call. I couldn't tear my eyes away from the damn thing. My legs twitched as I tapped my fingers on my knees over and over again, every muscle of my body poised and ready to spring into action the moment my phone rang.

I was so intent on waiting for the call that I almost missed it. The phone buzzed on and on as I watched it, my eyes sightless and my brain so over-stimulated that it had crashed. It was only after blinking a few times that I noticed it was Eli.

Quickly, I picked it up. "Is she okay? Is she okay? Is Ma okay—" My voice was as tightly wound as my body.

"I'm on my way to the hospital with her right now," Eli cut in. His voice was level and calming, but underneath it, I could hear the fear.

Oh, no. This isn't good.

"Wh-what happened, Eli?"

There was a pause. "She was unconscious on the floor. She has a good gash on her head. Don't worry. She's breathing. I'll be at the hospital soon. I'll call you when I know more."

"Eli—"

"Can't talk. Weather's too bad. Have to concentrate on the road."

The way his voice came out in short, clipped statements drove the point home. The storm over Frazier Falls was dangerous, and Eli was driving in it because of me.

I struggled to contain the fluctuations in my voice. "Okay. Thanks, Eli."

"Emily, I ..." He paused. "You should get yourself to the airport. Get on the first flight you can."

Those final sentences washed over me like an ice bath. They left me cold and numb. I knew what the underlying meaning of his words was. *My mother might not make it.*

Choking back a sob, I threw together an overnight bag and ran out to my car, but my hands were trembling so hard, I couldn't start the engine. I didn't know what to do. I couldn't drive like this, and Sadie had gone out for drinks with her friends. She'd be halfway sloshed by now.

I called Don.

It took a few rings before he picked up, but when he did, his voice was full of concern. "Is it your mother, Emily?"

"She—my friend went to check on her and found her uncon-scious on the floor. He's taking her to the hospital now."

It felt bizarre to call Eli my friend. We had never just been friends, had we? But I couldn't think about that now.

"What do you need me to do?" He asked in a gentle voice.

"Can you—can you take me to the airport? I can't stop shaking. I can't stop crying. I can't drive like this."

"Of course." There were a few seconds of silence before he added on, "They won't have any flights until the storm passes.

Wouldn't it be better to stay in your apartment until then? I could keep you company until—"

"No," I interrupted. "I'd rather be at the airport. I won't be able … if I sit at home, it will feel like I'm doing nothing."

"I understand. I'll be there in fifteen minutes. Don't go anywhere, okay?"

"I won't. I'll be out front in my car."

I sat in my car sobbing in the driver's seat while my shoulders shook, and my insides trembled. I couldn't stop blaming myself. My mother's health had only been getting worse. She and I both knew that. I thought I was doing the right thing by staying in Los Angeles, but in hindsight, I knew I was wrong. I stayed for the money to provide her with the things she needed, but what she really needed was me. If she died, I'd never be able to see her again. If she died, I'd never forgive myself.

Regardless of the circumstances under which I left Frazier Falls, I still left. I was halfway to being able to afford that generator, but what would it matter if mom wasn't there to use it.

"I've been so stupid," I cried out, the words barely audible around the tears in my throat.

All I could hope for was that Eli would get my mother to the hospital in time and save her. He could have so easily refused to answer my call—he'd have had every right to—and yet he hadn't. He picked up the phone because it was me. He didn't lecture me, or shout, or sneer at me. He didn't think to suggest that whatever I was dealing with wasn't his problem.

No, he immediately sprang to action as soon as he knew what was going on. Even if I had been overreacting, and my mother had been fine, Eli would never have angrily turned on me for wasting his time.

If I had stayed in Frazier Falls like I should have done in the first place, then the two of us could have been happy together. No, we would have. There were no two ways about it. The only thing that had made our relationship anything less than a proverbial match made in heaven had been my job, and my inability to tell him what was in my heart.

As I waited for Don to arrive, I talked myself into a life in Frazier Falls. I could find a job. Taking over for Rachel Wilkes would be a gift to the entire town.

And now that I had started getting to know some people like John Reilly and my mom's friend Lucy, I had to admit that Frazier Falls wasn't as awful as I had made it out to be. It was like my mom described, the town was bigger than home and smaller than Los Angeles. It was the right size. I was only beginning to understand what she meant now that it might be too late.

"I'm so stupid!" I yelled out again, banging my head against the steering wheel. Suddenly, a sharp rap on the window alerted me to Don's presence. He took one look at my face and opened the door, hugging me before I had an opportunity to say anything.

"Stop crying," he said. "It'll be fine. Let's get you in my car."

Neither of us said anything for most of the drive to the airport. I was drained, and I didn't think I could utter any words, even if I wanted to. When we arrived, Don led me to a seat before heading into one of the shops. When he returned, he collapsed beside me and handed over a bottle of water.

"You should eat, but something tells me you don't have an appetite right now, so drink and take some painkillers." He handed me two aspirin. "I have no doubt a massive headache is coming your way after all that crying."

I let out a humorless laugh. "No doubt."

He glanced at me. "I'm sure your mom will be okay."

"I don't know," I whispered, looking up at the high ceilings of the airport. Unshed tears clung to my eyes, causing the lights above me to blur and blend into one another. "This might be it. I have to consider that."

"Emily …"

"No, it's okay. Well, it's not. I should have been there. There were so many reasons for me to stay."

Don smiled. "You're right, but hindsight is always 20/20."

"Yes, and much clearer when you're looking from above. I messed everything up."

"I take it Frazier Falls isn't as awful as you thought?"

I dropped my head. "It was before I opened my eyes and saw how beautiful it could be. Can you really hate a place when the people who are most important to you live there?"

"I suppose not. In which case, I have a suggestion."

I turned my face slightly to look at him. His expression was sad even though he was smiling.

"What is it?"

He sighed. "I think … I think you should take a couple of years off."

"What?"

"I'm serious. I think you should quit your job and go live with your mom until … well, you know. Clearly, this incident has taught you which order your priorities are in, which frankly, is the right order. There's no way your mom will come to Los Angeles?"

I shook my head. "She loves where she lives. The air is clear, and she has friends. The weather is generally great. Not that this winter was representative of the norm."

"Damn global warming."

I couldn't help but cry some more. Don immediately put a hand on my shoulder.

"Emily …?"

"It's meant to be a joke when people say that. Damn global warming, as if it's the punchline to everything that goes wrong.

But the punchline is the fact that global warming could be the culprit."

"Frazier Falls might be subject to more aggressive storms in the next few years."

"Exactly."

"That's even more reason for you to leave Los Angeles to be with her."

"It's more than my mom."

"Your relationship with Eli Cooper?"

My jaw dropped. "How do know?"

He gave me an are-you-kidding look. "Sadie."

"Figures." I glanced at him through wet lashes. "Will you be okay if I leave?"

He shrugged. "I was never supposed to hire two people in the first place, remember? You and Sadie were so outstanding that I couldn't possibly have one of you snatched up by some other city, much to Pete's displeasure."

I laughed. "So, what are you saying?"

"I'm saying, I'll crack the whip and make Sadie pull her weight. You don't have to worry about us. Focus on spending as much time with your mom as you possibly can, okay? Try to make things work with that man of yours. He sounds like a good one."

We were interrupted by the sound of my phone. I'd taken it off vibrate for the first time in years, setting the call alert volume to high to make sure I didn't miss the next call. The shrill of the ring shocked me so much that I jumped out of my chair before fumbling for the phone.

When I saw Eli's name, even though it was who I desperately wanted to hear from, I couldn't answer the call.

"What's wrong, Emily?" A frown marred Don's face.

"I'm scared."

"Of what the hospital will say?"

I nodded. "What if …"

He reached over and took my phone out of my hand, accepting the call for me.

"This is Emily's phone. Don speaking."

I couldn't hear what Eli was saying in response, but as soon as Don smiled reassuringly at me, I let out a huge sigh of relief and grabbed the phone back.

"Eli, it's me. What's going on?"

"Why is your boss screening your calls?"

I laughed at how absurd it sounded. He sounded jealous.

"I didn't—I was too scared to answer."

"You're ridiculous, do you know that?"

"I know. I'm sorry. What's going on?"

"The doctors think she has the flu. I called Lucy, and it seems as if your mom had been feeling poorly, but insisted it was nothing. Turns out, she was weak and tried to get up but tripped over her oxygen tank. She knocked herself out good, but her condition is stable. She has a concussion and got a few stitches, but she should be okay."

"You're … you're sure?"

"As sure as I can be. Don't worry. I won't leave her side until you get here, so don't die from worry in the meantime."

"That's a cruel thing to say."

"What, that I'll stay by her side? I thought that was me being nice. A gentleman, even."

Before I knew it, I was laughing again. "You're the only gentleman I know who tells a woman not to die in the meantime."

"Clearly, you don't know many gentlemen."

My heart warmed with his kindness. "Thank you, Eli."

"It's not a problem. Let me know as soon as there's a flight available, okay? I'll let you know if anything changes."

"Thank you, and Eli?" I waited a breath. "We need to talk when I get to the hospital. Talk about us because there is an us."

"You bet your sweet ass we do. Night, Emily."

"Night, Eli."

Once I hung up, a wave of understanding crossed Don's face. "If you needed another reason to leave Los Angeles, it's right there, in that call?"

Suddenly, I felt embarrassed. "Eli Cooper. He—"

"Is he related to Owen? The one who runs the Green House Project?"

"Yes. He's one of Owen's younger brothers."

At that moment, it looked like Don had a flash of inspiration.

"Your project proposal could do with a trial somewhere smaller than Los Angeles. The data derived could sell his plan to big cities across the globe. Are they implementing anything in Frazier Falls?"

CHAPTER TWENTY-THREE

ELI

J udy was in stable condition. The doctors had put her on a
strong course of antibiotics to clear up the infection and
stitched up the cut on her head.

I hoped to God that Emily would be able to get to Colorado
soon. Nobody was actually sure if the storm had been the primary
cause of Judy's collapse, but I deduced that she had no lights and
had tripped over her oxygen tank.

The doctors were fairly certain she had contracted a late-
season winter flu, but given that she was also responding to antibiotics, it was possible that there was something else at work that
wasn't a virus. Lying in a cold, dark house on her own for several
hours had certainly not helped.

I hadn't left the hospital once, instead, relying on my brothers
to bring me a change of clothes and a meal. I couldn't imagine
anything worse than Judy waking up to an empty room. It
wouldn't be what I'd want, which was company, and lots of it.

I left Judy's bedside in search of a cup of coffee. It was bitter and cheap-tasting, but it was coffee, nonetheless. The caffeine hit me, taking the edge away from my exhaustion.

Pax had been in contact with Lucy Rogers to keep her informed of Judy's progress. The younger woman had wanted to visit her in the hospital, but given the storm that started as rain and turned to sleet, then to snow, it was simply too risky.

John Reilly had called too, as had Rachel Wilkes. It was gratifying that even in the middle of a storm, there were many people concerned enough about Judy Flanagan's health that they would gladly brave the weather to see her. Even Alice sent pie.

Sadly, the most important person couldn't make it through the storm to see Judy. I had wondered for a panic-stricken moment if Emily might try to tackle the long drive from Los Angeles to Frazier Falls, but even she wouldn't risk that. She was in no state to get behind the wheel going by the fact that she had asked her boss to take her to the airport.

It had been a few hours since I'd heard from her, though I figured she had probably fallen asleep. Because of the wildly varying times that she had messaged and called me over the last twelve hours, it would come as absolutely no surprise if she was out for the count. Hopefully, she was on a plane, or in a taxi coming from the airport.

Not for the first time, had I wished that I could be by her side to comfort her. Her boss, Don, had been there for her. A stab of jealousy poked at me when I thought about him. He'd been there for her when I wasn't. I cradled my head and swallowed the regret.

"I'm an idiot," I muttered in irritation.

Behind me, a nurse taking care of Judy laughed.

"Mr. Cooper, don't worry. Ms. Flanagan is doing well. Her pain meds will wear off soon, and she should wake up in the next hour or so. Will you stay with her until then?"

I nodded and went back to Judy's room. The old woman before me looked frail as if she might wither away to nothing under the fluorescent, unforgiving light of the hospital, but there was some color to her cheeks that hadn't been there when I'd brought her in.

"I wish Emily was here for you," I whispered, reaching out to hold her hand. "You and I both know how hard she's working to get back."

A few minutes later, Judy shifted in her sleep. I could see her eyes roving underneath their lids. Her eyelashes fluttered, and I felt the pressure of her hand squeezing mine.

She opened her eyes as a human-shaped cannonball rushed through the door.

Emily, with her hair in disarray and her puffy cheeks as red as apples, breathed heavily as she clutched the doorframe. She glanced at me for half a second, then widened her eyes when Judy smiled at her.

"Emily, sweetheart, why do you look like you ran a marathon?" Judy asked quietly. Her voice was barely a croak.

I held up a cup of water with a straw in it, which Judy drank from before realizing who had given it to her.

"Eli? What am I—" She looked around the room. "Where am I?"

Her question was left unanswered as Emily hurled herself forward; her body wracked with sobs as she collapsed onto the bed, her arms circling her mother before another word could be said.

"Emily, honey, what happened? I'm okay; you're okay," Judy soothed. She looked at me. "Eli, could you tell me what happened?"

I smiled softly, which hid the tightness I felt as I recalled what had happened. "It looks like you tripped and fell," I explained. "Emily was worried about you because of the weather, and you hadn't returned her calls, so she asked me to check up on you. I found you on the floor and took you to the hospital. That was yesterday."

"Yesterday? Oh, my. I remember not feeling well. My cough was coming back. I stood up …" Judy shrugged.

"How are you feeling now?" I asked.

"Much, much better. Thank you for bringing me to the hospital. Have you been here the whole time?"

I nodded, suddenly embarrassed. "I didn't want you to be alone when you woke up."

Judy beamed. "Your parents clearly brought you up right. Emily, stop crying and look at me. Can't you see I'm okay?"

"You didn't tell me you were feeling worse," Emily cried against the pillow. Her mother smiled down at her, stroking Emily's beautiful red hair. "You can't do that. I need to know these things. Otherwise …"

"Okay. I swear I won't do it again. I didn't want you to worry."

Emily looked up suddenly, her eyes wet and bright. "You won't get a chance to do it again. I'm moving to Frazier Falls."

Judy frowned. "Honey, don't do this for—"

"For what? Don't do this for you? Ma, you're the most important person in the world to me. And I—I nearly lost you. It was horrible, not being able to be by your side. I won't let that happen again."

"But what about your job?"

Emily wiped away the tears on her face and sat up on the bed.

I got out of the chair I was sitting on to let her take it instead, but Emily shook her head.

"Some things are more important, Ma." She looked between her mom and me. "The people I love are important. I'm staying. As long as the store has potatoes, we won't starve."

Judy laughed, but then winced. "That was a sentence I never thought I'd hear." Then she glanced over at me, sitting silently and politely and waiting for—I didn't know what. Had Emily just said in a roundabout way that she loved me? I suddenly became aware of the fact that it wasn't right for me to be interrupting this moment.

I stood up. "I'll be outside if you need me."

Judy looked at her daughter. "Emily, why don't you go and grab some food with Eli, he must be starving. Maybe you can sneak me in a burger."

"No burgers, Ma. Maybe some broth." Emily looked at me. "Are you hungry?"

I was hungry. Hungry for her kisses, her touch, and her words. I held the door open. There was a small smile on her face as she mouthed 'such a gentleman' to me. I bit back a laugh.

We spotted the doctor in the corridor, so I asked him to check in on Judy before both Emily and I headed for the cafeteria. When we walked past an empty room, she pulled me into it instead.

"What are you doing?" I asked in a hushed voice as she closed the door behind us.

Her bright eyes bored right through me. "I don't need food right now. Okay, I do, but not as much as I need to talk to you first."

"We don't need to do this right this second."

"Yes, we do. I do. Eli, I'm so incredibly sorry for how I left Frazier Falls. It wasn't fair. And you were right; I wasn't being honest."

I looked down at her as she tucked an errant strand of hair behind her ear, which fell back in front of her face as soon as she pulled her hand away. I brushed it back with my hand and kept my hand on her cheek. Emily gasped in surprise at the gesture.

"You haven't done anything that needs forgiving," I said, keeping my voice even.

Emily raised an eyebrow. "But I have. I was wrong."

I cocked my head to the side, still catching up with the conversation. "Did you say you were wrong?"

"Of course, that's what you'd hear."

I chuckled. "We were both at fault. I'm as much to blame. I knew what the answers to all of my questions were already. I was the immature one for forcing you to answer them out loud when we both knew how painful those answers would be. I wanted something from you that you couldn't give me. Can you forgive me?"

Emily nuzzled her face against my hand. I gently stroked the edge of her jaw with my thumb, feeling as if every ounce of exhaustion had left my body to be abruptly replaced by another feeling entirely.

"Forgiven," Emily said, as she turned her face into my hand and kissed my palm.

I bent down to rest my forehead against hers. "What's this about you moving to Frazier Falls?"

A smile blossomed on her lips. "Turns out, it's not as dismal here as I thought. Maybe there are one or two people here that I like."

I grinned, sliding my arms around her waist to pull her in closer. "Maybe?"

"Okay, definitely."

"You don't feel any regret about having to move?"

She shook her head. "None, I'm where I need to be—where I want to be."

"In an empty hospital room with me?"

She glanced behind me, pushing me forward slightly with her body.

"There's a bed. What more do we need?"

I ran one of my hands up her back to her neck, my fingers gently clutching at her hair in order to pull her face up. I kissed her, softly at first, then harder. By the time I felt the edge of the bed hit my back, our kiss was ferocious, the two of us desperate for each other.

"Nothing, I need nothing," I said as Emily hugged me tightly. "Nothing at all."

I leaned against the bed, pulling her into my lap. She dug her hands into my back, underneath the fabric of my shirt, while my hands slid over her hips.

"I want you to make love to me." The breathless, lustful plea was the most beautiful sound I'd ever heard.

I chuckled, my voice soft and low, "Did you forget what it felt like to be together?"

She bit my upper lip, her eyes heavy-lidded and mischievous.

"I could never forget what perfect felt like."

I kissed her, long, hard, and lingering as my hands clutched at her bottom, and my insides coiled within me, desperate for more.

I pulled away and smiled. "How about I remind you daily?"

"Promise?"

"That can be arranged. Better make it worth my while, though, Flanagan."

She widened her eyes in mock outrage. "Excuse me?"

And there it was,—that phrase that had so infuriated me upon first meeting Emily Flanagan, but that now sounded beautiful leaving her lush lips.

"I love you, you know," I said, matter-of-factly.

Emily raised an eyebrow. "You do, do you?"

I kissed her neck, pressing my teeth in enough to hear her gasp.

"Do you not want to know if I love you, too?" she asked, her voice breathless.

"You said so when you asked me to make love to you, which I will do as soon as I get you to my bed."

She entangled her fingers in my hair and pulled my mouth back to hers.

"I guess I did."

CHAPTER TWENTY-FOUR

EMILY

Early April in Frazier Falls was beautiful. The warm spring sunshine coaxed the flowers and trees to bud and bloom. Everything was green and blue and yellow, with no snow or rain in sight.

It was a world away from the hellish winter that had battered the town into March. There wasn't a single person in Frazier Falls who would wish that winter upon anyone. It had been too severe to comprehend fully. The damage it dealt to people's houses, and the parks, and trees, and roads, as well as people's health, had been extensive. It would take a long time to recover from it all.

However, Cooper Construction was doing a damn fine job of whittling away at the first two problems on their own.

Nearly all on their own.

"Flanagan, come over here for a moment."

"Hold your horses, Owen," I called back, putting down the plans I'd been looking at.

He waved me over to a scale-model house based on my mother's floor plan.

"How do you think this looks?" he asked. "If we go in right underneath the porch, we won't have to dig up too much of the foundation. It'll probably take longer to install the underground heating system this way, but it will minimize the nuisance to your mother while we do it."

I smiled. "It looks great. What about the solar panels? Ma's house isn't south-facing, and it's got some pretty large trees around it."

"Already sorted. We're going to put them on rotational platforms, so they'll move to catch the sun."

"Oh, like a sunflower?"

He smiled. "That was the inspiration. Might take your mom a while to get used to them sticking out of her roof like an alien antenna, but she will."

I had one final question. "What about the—"

"Yes, we'll put in a backup generator while we work on the new heating system. Don't worry, Emily."

"Can't exactly blame me."

He chuckled. "I guess not. How is the park design going? Do you have all the specs I need, yet?"

"Nearly," I replied. "I'm trying to integrate a small kitchen into the building plan if I can."

Owen raised an eyebrow. "A kitchen?"

"Yes, in case anyone gets caught in bad weather, or a kid gets lost. They could make a cup of tea or get some juice and snacks while they wait to be picked up."

"And how do we prevent people from simply going in and stealing all the food?"

I shrugged. "An honesty system?" It didn't seem like a stretch in a small town like Frazier Falls, where everyone looked after each other. Or I should say, the Cooper brothers looked after everyone.

"Keep working on it, and I'll figure out how to implement it. It's not a huge space, after all. Maybe running water and a microwave?"

Eli leaned against the doorway of Owen's office, watching the two of us with amusement. "Can I have my girlfriend back? I swear you spend more time with her than I do."

"I agree," came Carla's voice from behind him.

It was true, ever since Owen brought me on as an Urban planning consultant, the amount of work had doubled. Big cities were afraid to take the plunge, but with me on board to answer questions, it wasn't as risky.

"Owen," Carla said. "We have a meeting with the caterer, remember?"

Owen's eyes widened immediately as he rushed out of his seat. "I absolutely didn't forget. Let's go, and we can grab an early dinner afterward?"

They left, leaving Eli and me inside Owen's office. He walked over and kissed me lightly.

"I don't spend more time with Owen on purpose, but it's natural that I spend a lot of time with him at work, since, you know, we're working together."

He laughed as he took my hand, leading me out of the office and back over to the desk that had become mine. The desk that sat right next to Eli's.

"I know," he admitted. "I wish I had a clue what the two of you were discussing so I could join in, but it's above my pay grade."

"Or your intelligence," Pax called out.

Eli gave him the finger while I giggled behind his back.

"On that note, I need to get back to work," I said. "Don wanted an update on the progress I've made so far." Since I'd moved to Colorado, Pete had increased his interest in the Green House

Project, which meant Don and I were working together again, but in a different capacity. I still worked for him, but that was because he was a client. Los Angeles fully intended to put the Green House Project to work in its new urban renewal plan.

"But I asked you yesterday to take this afternoon off."

I quirked an eyebrow. "I didn't think you were serious."

"And what part of my request wasn't serious?"

"I figured you weren't thinking clearly," I leaned in and whispered, "since we were pretty naked at the time of the request and—"

"Naked?"

"Oh God, don't give Pax any more cannon fodder," Eli shivered. "He's bad enough as it is, but I did actually want to take you somewhere."

"Okay, you have my interest. Where do you want to take me?"

"It's a surprise."

I rolled my eyes. "Can't it wait until I've finished the report?"

"I thought the report wasn't due until next week."

"Do you listen to all my conversations?"

"Baby, I hang on your every word."

"Especially when I'm chatting with Don," I said, amused, as I turned off my laptop, cleaned up my desk, and grabbed my denim jacket from the back of my chair.

Eli spluttered incoherently for a few moments. "Not true," he protested.

"Aw, you jealous of her old boss, Eli?" Paxton teased from his corner of the office.

"Give it a rest." He looked at me. "I'm not jealous of Don, exactly. It's just …"

"Just what?"

"You never told me how good-looking he was."

"Is that an issue? Surely you should be grateful that I never thought enough about how good-looking he was to bring it up in the first place."

"Oh, she's got you there, Eli," Paxton teased.

"Shut up."

"It doesn't matter if he's good-looking or not," I continued. "I think Don has more interest in being my dad than anything else."

"Kinky."

"Paxton," I warned. "You're pushing it." For a brother who was known as the town mute, he sure had a lot to say lately.

"Come on, let's head out." Eli took my hand, and he led me outside.

We drove in his truck for a few minutes before he glanced at me and asked, "So, how is it working out? Are you enjoying your job? Owen can be a bit intense when it comes to his design work."

"Oh, no, Owen is great," I replied enthusiastically. "He's wonderful to work with and has such good ideas. He implements everything I need as naturally as if he came up with the requirements himself. I'm glad his work is gaining recognition."

"Should I be jealous of my brother rather than your old boss?"

I ignored his comment. "With Frazier Falls as town zero, I think we're looking at a pretty successful trial of my ecological redevelopment plan."

He hesitated before asking, "Do you think you'll ever want to move back to Los Angeles to help them implement the plan? I mean, this was your idea."

"I'll have to go back soon." I watched his face fall. "To get my stuff. Now that I've stayed here long enough to enjoy it, I don't know how I ever managed to live in the city for so long. I feel much … healthier here. Not just physically."

Eli's smile grew bright. "That's probably because you don't have to worry about your mother being a thousand miles away anymore."

"Probably." I glanced at him. "I don't think that's the only reason."

"Oh?"

"Yeah, I think a certain someone's companionship has made me realize how lonely I was in California."

Eli surprised me by laughing loudly.

"What?"

"You're only realizing that now?"

"Yeah, why?"

He shook his head. "No, it's nothing, just ... spending time with you made me realize how lonely I'd been after three days. And it took you three months? God, that's a long time to lie to yourself."

"You're right again. Are we close to where we're going?"

"Almost," Eli replied as he turned a corner and passed by his house.

"I thought there wasn't much up this path except another road into the forest?"

"There wasn't—past tense."

"And there is now?"

"Wait and see."

I sat in the passenger seat impatiently as Eli seemed to drive as slowly as possible along the road that hugged the Cooper side of the forest. The large oak trees were beginning to unfurl their spring leaves.

I rolled down the window an inch or so in order to enjoy the sounds of the birds singing, and to feel the warmth from a beam of sunlight shining on my face.

I closed my eyes, thinking about how gorgeous the forest was.

The car suddenly stopped, startling me out of my newfound Zen state. I opened my eyes and looked at Eli.

"We're here?"

He nodded, grinning, "Yes, we're here."

I got out of the car and followed him down a winding path that led into the forest.

"Where are we going?"

"Hold on a minute more. The road isn't finished yet, we can't drive all the way in, but in a week, that will change."

The end of the path spilled into a clearing, where a house seemed to melt into the forest. It was a beautiful, understated piece of architecture. It looked like it had grown from the earth on which it was built.

"Eli, this is … wow. Did Owen design it?"

"Yes. This one is my favorite."

He held my hand once more and walked me inside. "It's built using lumber from the forest, and local stone. All the windows act as solar panels. The whole thing is state-of-the-art, but from the outside, it looks like a log cabin. My brother pulled out all the stops for this one."

I glanced up at him. "Did you bring me here to brag about your brother? Not that I mind …" I walked up the steps. "Can I take a peek inside? I do enjoy peeping inside other people's houses."

"You can go in, Emily, because it's ours."

I paused with my hand on the door handle of the perfect wooden house. "Excuse me?"

"It's ours. If you want to be with me, that is. I've wanted to sell my current place and move into one of Owen's eco-homes for a while, and I figured you probably didn't want to stay in your mom's house forever."

He opened the door and led me into the center of the room, where he'd already placed a bottle of wine, a candle, and a blanket.

I turned around to face him, a small smile lifting my lips. "Are you sure you can handle living with someone like me?"

He bent down and kissed me. "I know I can't handle living without you."

I looked around at the beauty of the hardwood floors, the pale cream walls, and the forest beyond the windows.

This town had become everything. It was more than a community. More than my home. With Eli by my side, it was my future.

My mom once said I had to make big decisions for love. In the end, I knew that loving Eli was the easiest decision I'd ever make.

SNEAK PEEK INTO DEFEND ME

PAXTON

There's a reason we're born with two ears and one mouth. We're supposed to listen more than we talk. If there was one thing I knew with absolute certainty, it was that I learned a whole lot more about what was going on around me if I kept quiet and paid attention.

"Paxton, do you want the usual?" Alice breezed toward me, pad in hand and a pen sticking out of her poof of hair.

I'd commandeered my brother's booth for the moment knowing he wasn't going to show up. "Yes, coffee and apple pie, please."

"Coming up." She leaned a hip on the chipped Formica table. "Where are those brothers of yours?"

"Not here."

"Obviously." Alice popped me on the head with her pad and walked away.

My brothers were at Reilly's waiting for me. That's what I wanted to believe, but the reality was they'd be at Reilly's with their significant others and not notice my absence. Their pairing up would leave me the fifth wheel or worse, Rich's date, which was always awkward because he wasn't my type.

As the youngest brother of the three Coopers I didn't need to say much, but razzing Alice was a requirement. She was like family and exempt from my silence.

I turned my ears to the chatter surrounding me. Growing up, I enjoyed listening to other people. In most circumstances someone would always say what I'd been thinking, saving me from voicing my opinion. What was the point of repeating what everyone already knew?

Several people in the diner were discussing my brother Owen and Carla. Their wedding was fast approaching and was the talk of the town. Nothing quite as exciting had happened in Frazier Falls since the avalanche in ninety-seven—eighteen ninety-seven.

The knitting club was crammed into the corner booth betting on the type of flowers they'd have and whether Carl would wear white.

"She's no virgin," Isabel Walker shouted a bit too loud, which drew the stares of many. She dropped her knitting needles and shook her head.

"Hell, these days, kids are born with experience." Scarlet Lewellen pulled out another ball of yarn and continued her work on what looked like a pair of baby booties. "Miriam's granddaughter is a baby having a baby and she marched to the altar eight months along and dressed in white."

Wanda Kraft looked over her shoulder at me. "There's one left. Who do you think Paxton will end up with?"

My mouth dropped open. They were talking about me.

"Maybe he'll meet his match at the ceremony."

The entire group turned toward me and one by one they raised their hands and waved.

"Maybe he'll catch the garter which would mean he'd be next."

I shook my head and made a mental note to avoid the garter at all costs.

"Here you go." Alice slid a plate of pie and a coffee on the table. I swear she always gave me a double portion.

"It's too bad you're taken, Alice. A woman who can make pie like you might be able to enter my heart."

Down came the order pad on my head again. "She's out there waiting for you, Pax. Never say never."

"Never," I said before I shoved my mouth full of pie.

"Someone, someday, will earn their place in your warm, smooshy soul. You're a Teddy bear destined to be hugged and cherished. If you weren't so busy catering to all the widows in town, you might have time to find a woman for yourself."

"I love those cougars." There was nothing going on between me and the senior residents of Frazier Falls. I liked to be helpful and found my niche assisting the older folks of my little town.

"Between work and Lucy Rogers, you may never find a mate. Although there's a table of interesting women giving you a look over now." We both glanced at the knitters in the corner.

"Not looking for one." I loved the term she used, because while I liked the mating part, I wasn't that good at all the rest.

Alice trotted off in her red high-top sneakers while I reflected on my existence. I enjoyed working with my brothers. Cooper Construction was a successful business, and with Owen's Green House project taking off, we were beginning to garner a good reputation across the globe. It was rewarding to do good work and be recognized as an industry leader in green living. Though Owen was the one who designed his eco-friendly houses, I was the one responsible for much of the building of them and the running of the company.

It had always worked well. Owen was the architect. Eli was the numbers guy. When we got on-site, the responsibility fell to me to ensure the actual construction work got done.

It was the way I liked it. Good, honest, physically hard work left my mind free to wander. It also meant that I never had to take work home like my brothers. My free time was filled by helping others with tasks they couldn't always do themselves. I didn't know when or why I'd started doing this, but it filled me with a deep sense of satisfaction that I didn't get from anything else.

Alice's comment about helping others taking up too much of my time was dead wrong. It was actually a time saver. Because I wouldn't accept compensation, everyone showed their appreciation with homemade food. I might starve if not for Lucy Rogers, Judy Flanagan, and a half dozen others who cooked me casseroles and roasts and baked goods in large quantities.

I finished my pie and laid down a ten to pay before I walked out and headed to the bar to meet my brothers for a beer.

I no sooner walked inside when John Reilly handed me a Tupperware container. "Thank you again for all your help over winter with the restocking," He nodded toward my brothers and Emily, who sat at the end of the bar. "They're only a half a pint ahead of you."

"I'm a coffee and a piece of pie ahead of them."

"Smart man. Eat before you drink."

I looked down at the gift of food from John. "Irish stew?"

"Yes, with extra carrots just the way you like it."

"You're the best." I tucked the container under my arm and moved toward the group. Carla and her brother Rich hadn't arrived yet.

I glanced at Eli. "I've got Irish stew if you want to join me after our beer."

My brother shook his head and wrapped his arm around his girlfriend's shoulder. "Emily and I already have plans."

"I know what that means," Owen laughed. "They're going to indulge in a different appetite."

"I'm not discussing my sex life with you," Eli muttered. He turned to me before adding, "I'm happy to take that off your hands though. I'm sure you've got plenty of similar dishes filling your refrigerator and freezer." Eli looked at Emily. "We'll have to come up for air and forage for food at some point."

She gave him a solid slug in the arm. "You said you weren't talking about our sex life."

A smile curled my lips. "Nope, I'll have no problem eating it all on my own. Reilly's Irish stew is amazing."

"You pig," Eli called out.

I shrugged my shoulders, indifferent to the insult.

Owen looked at me. "Mind if I steal some for Carla and me?"

"I'll bring it over to your place and we can share the meal," I said.

Eli pouted. "Why share with him?"

"Because he didn't call me a pig."

"Nope, not out loud anyway," Owen chimed in as Carla and her brother Rich walked into the bar. "That wasn't an invite to join us, it was a request for food."

I slapped a hand over my heart. "I'm wounded."

Carla kissed Owen's cheek as he handed her a beer.

"Pax offered to bring us his dinner. Irish stew compliments of John."

She looked at the container and me. "Can I take the stew and pass on the visit? I love you brother-to-be, but I've got plans for Owen and they don't call for a chaperone."

"Geez, I swear you're going to wear yourselves out before the honeymoon." I looked from Owen and Carla to Eli and Emily trying to make a point. "See what happens when you set a date? It's like a race to the finish and once you're married—"

Emily broke in. "That's why Eli and I have no intention of getting married any time soon. We need lots of practice."

Eli looked at her. "Now who's talking?" He gave me a tap. "I'd say get a girlfriend so you're not so lonely, but I fear that would be an impossible task."

"Rude." It was true, though. I had dated women in the past, but I'd never had a serious girlfriend before. I didn't want one. Women were … complicated. Often chatty and I wasn't good with expressing my emotions. I didn't say any of this to my present company because I knew that both Emily and Carla would pull my ear for hours explaining the benefits of a girlfriend.

"Pax, get your head back in the conversation," Owen said.

"I was never out of it," I replied smoothly. I pointed to the group. "Don't forget your roles. You're the talkers, I'm the listener. Want to quiz me? I can repeat anything you've ever told me. Can't answer to the things you haven't."

By their expressions, they knew I was referring to Owen's panic attacks. Particularly the one he had at the architectural exhibit where I discovered that Eli had known about Owen's anxiety problems for years, and I'd been kept in the dark.

Before that, I'd assumed we never spoke about such things because there was nothing to talk about. Now I knew we were all idiots who probably needed to open up to each other more often. "You want a word-by-word retelling?" They knew I could do it. Eli scowled while the rest of the group laughed.

"Did you have a look at the plans I sent you for the wedding venue?" Owen abruptly changed the topic of conversation.

I suppressed a scowl. "Yes."

"And …?"

"And that's a hell of a lot of work you want me to do."

"Come on," Owen protested. "You're the only person I know who could build what we need as quickly as we need it."

"No, I'm the only one you know of who will do it for free."

"May as well keep it in the family, right?"

I sighed with resignation.

"You already knew I'd do it, so don't act as if you were giving me a choice."

Carla squealed with delight as she hugged me. "Thanks, Pax. You're a lifesaver."

"Building it on top of the creek will be complicated," I warned. "The design is more elaborate than it needs to be. Simple and sturdy will keep you all dry."

Owen laughed. "I'll keep that in mind."

The rest of the evening passed by in an easy conversation that I was happy to listen to. Aside from a sarcastic comment here or there, I had no need to speak up, which sat perfectly in my lane.

As I leaned back and watched my brothers, I thought about how complicated their lives had become. What used to be a Friday night beer with siblings was a coordinating of schedules nightmare. We used to talk about chicks and now the only topic of conversation was flower choices, types of cake, and tuxedo fittings.

I would happily live my life without those problems.

I left the bar alone knowing that single was spectacular—or at least that was my story and I was sticking to it.

Click here to read more.

NEED MORE SMALL TOWN ROMANCE?

An Aspen Cove Romance Series

One Hundred Reasons

One Hundred Heartbeats

One Hundred Wishes

One Hundred Promises

One Hundred Excuses

One Hundred Christmas Kisses

One Hundred Lifetimes

One Hundred Ways

One Hundred Goodbyes

One Hundred Secrets

One Hundred Regrets

One Hundred Choices

To see more Kelly Collins' books go to www.authorkellycollins.com

GET A FREE BOOK.

Go to www.authorkellycollins.com

ABOUT THE AUTHOR

International bestselling author of more than thirty novels, Kelly Collins writes with the intention of keeping the love alive. Always a romantic, she blends real-life events with her vivid imagination to create characters and stories that lovers of contemporary romance, new adult, and romantic suspense will return to again and again.

Kelly lives in Colorado at the base of the Rocky Mountains with her husband of twenty-nine years, their dog Sophie, a cat name Ginger, and a green cheeked conure named Rosco. She has three amazing children, whom she loves to pieces.

For More Information
www.authorkellycollins.com
kelly@authorkellycollins.com

Made in the USA
Middletown, DE
12 January 2020